REMIND ME

SAMANTHA CHASE

Editor: Jillian Rivera

Cover Design: Uplifting Designs/Alyssa Garcia

PROLOGUE

Six Years Ago...

Mallory skipped down the steps and breathed in the ocean air and smiled. No doubt she was going to miss all of this, but it had been a good summer – a great summer! And the memories of it would get her through until she could come back.

Things between her and Jake weren't the best. After their wild romp on the boathouse roof almost a week ago, things were strained and he was distant. They said their goodbyes last night. He said it would be for the best if he didn't come by this morning.

She had to agree.

Looking over her shoulder toward the path that led to his house, she was tempted to run over and see him one last time, but she knew he wasn't there. He was going to Wilmington today to visit some friends. And again, she had to remind herself that it was for the best. She already cried all night. There was no sense in making herself cry more while she drove.

Like that's not going to happen anyway...

Grabbing her phone, she ran back up to the house and straight to Pops' office. After another round of hugs, kisses, and promises to call when she got home, Mallory made her way down to her car and gave the big house one last look.

A long breath whooshed out as she started the car. "I'm coming back," she murmured. "This isn't goodbye and it isn't forever." And with those words, she slowly drove around the large, circular drive and made her way up to the road.

She hadn't gone more than a mile when she groaned.

"Dammit!" Immediately, she did a three-point turn and made her way back to Pops' house. "Darn phone charger." Berating herself for forgetting it, she shook her head. "As organized as I am, how could I have left it behind?"

The answer was simple – she'd brought it down to the boathouse yesterday and left it there by mistake. All morning she kept reminding herself to go down and get it, but between breakfast with Pops and saying goodbye, it slipped her mind.

Rather than going to the front door, Mallory pulled the car around to the Sound side of the house, since it was closer to the boathouse. No need to go inside and go through another round of goodbyes, right?

It took less than five minutes, but as she was heading back to her car, she spotted Jake walking up the back steps of the house and going into the kitchen. Was he coming to say goodbye to her before she left? Her heart skipped a beat and she giddily went after him.

Just one more kiss, she told herself. *One more kiss and I'll be able to handle anything.*

When she walked into the kitchen, he wasn't there.

Through the dining room, and he wasn't there.

Nope, not in the living room. What in the world?

In the distance, she heard voices. Jake was talking to Pops. She heard her name mentioned and while she felt a little bad about eavesdropping, she was a little curious if Jake would profess his love for her to her great-grandfather or – at the very least – say how much he was going to miss her.

"I hate this, Zeke. You know that."

"I know you do, but you'll do it because you know it's the right thing."

Silence.

"It shouldn't be like this...I hate lying."

Lying? What was he lying about? She thought.

"You're not lying, son. You're doing what you need to do."

"Am I? Because it feels like a lie. I should have talked to Mallory..."

"Leave Mallory out of this!" Pops snapped. "This has nothing to do with her and everything to do with you and your future. And if you actually want a future – a chance to make something of your life – then you're going to take this and go." He paused. "Don't look back, Jacob. You know this is what you need to do."

Her stomach clenched and she felt like her breakfast was about to make a reappearance. What was she supposed to do? What were they talking about? What was Jake lying about?

"Take the money and go," Pops said.

Oh, God! Pops was paying Jake to go away! How...why...?!

The little voice in her head kept telling her to move – to go confront the two of them – but she couldn't move, was almost paralyzed where she stood. And just when she thought she'd go mad, Jake stormed out of Pops' office, walking right toward her. Only...he didn't see her. He was looking at the ground and it wasn't until he bumped right into her that they both seemed to snap out of their inner thoughts.

"Mallory?" he cried, seemingly horrified at seeing her there. "What...I thought you were gone."

Her throat burned and she took a step back. "I was. I...I forgot my phone charger and came back for it." She paused and glared at him. "And I thought you were going to Wilmington."

He glanced away guiltily. "Yeah, well...I had to...um..."

"You know what?" she said with disgust. "It doesn't matter. Really. Clearly you've got your secrets and I don't mean enough to you to share them."

"Mallory..." he reached for her but she moved away.

"It's better this way," she said, hating how her voice shook. "Now I finally know where I stand." Taking another step back, she gave him one last look. "I think under these circumstances it would be best if we just called this what it was – a summer fling. Nothing serious, right?"

"Mallory, just give me a minute to explain!"

But she couldn't listen. Didn't want to. She had to leave. Now. Now, before she broke down and made even more of a fool out of herself than she had all summer long. "I need to go."

Then she was running down the hall and out the front door. She heard Pops call her name as she ran by his office but she didn't stop. Down the porch steps and across the gravel driveway, she didn't stop. Even when she got in the car, she quickly started it, threw it in gear and sped away.

This time she didn't look back at the big plantation house.

This really was goodbye.

And maybe forever…

———

The Next Morning…

"I expected more from you than to have you run away like that."

It was pointless to argue. Mallory had expected more from herself too. "I know," she replied softly.

"You heard a small portion of a conversation and reacted rather than getting the facts. Are you willing to sit and listen to them now?"

She nodded.

"Mallory?"

Oh, right. Pops couldn't see her nod through the phone. "I am."

"Jake didn't get his financial aid for school and he didn't want to burden his parents with helping him. I offered and he accepted," Pops explained in his usual no-nonsense way.

"Why didn't either of you tell me?" she demanded quietly, knowing better than to be disrespectful and yell at her great-grandfather.

"I can't speak for Jake, but I didn't think it was any of your business."

Yup. No-nonsense.

"Pops…"

"It's true, Mallory. If you had known there was an issue with Jake's tuition, are you telling me you wouldn't have tried to change his mind about going so far away for school?"

"Well…"

"You would," he said before she could answer. "I know how close the two of you were all summer and if you would have asked, Jake would have caved and done what you wanted to make you happy."

Was it wrong that she saw it as a good thing rather than a bad one?

"You and I both know it would have been wrong, Mallory," he said, as if reading her mind. "Jake lost out on a lot due to the financial struggles of his family. He's not a kid going away to college. He's a twenty-four-year-old man and he's waited long enough. I've offered him help in the past and he's always turned it down."

"Then why did he suddenly accept?" And yeah, her tone was a bit bratty, but she couldn't help it.

There was a weary sigh from the other end of the phone and she knew there was a bit of a lecture coming.

"The Summerfords have always been prideful, Mallory. All the years Jake's father was out of work and they hated getting a handout from anyone—no matter how much they needed it. That's what Jake learned growing up. He would have kept right on working for me at Coleman Construction and he might have even been happy doing it, but there's a lot more to that man and he deserves to discover that for himself."

"I know, Pops, I just wish..."

"No," he quickly interrupted.

"You don't even know what I was going to say!"

"You would have said how you still wished someone would have told you," he replied and dammit, he was right. That was exactly what she was going to say. "And I'm here to tell you that Jake needed to go with a clear conscience and to have his chance to finally do what he wants to do and make what he wants of his life without anyone's inter-ference."

She was about to point out that by Pops giving Jake the financing, he was interfering.

But she didn't.

"So you can be mad and you can pout all you want, missy," he scolded, "but the only one in the wrong then is you."

Again, it was on the tip of her tongue to argue, but she didn't.

"Now the way I see it, you need to call Jake and apolo-gize. He was a damn wreck after you left and I had to stop him from getting in his truck and chasing after you!"

"You...you did?"

"What good would it have done for him to get in the car when he was that upset? Someone would have had an acci-dent with the way he was behaving!"

Oh, God...what have I done?

She'd been home for less than twelve hours and had ignored any calls and texts that came through on her cell phone for the entire eleven-hour drive back to her home on Long Island from Magnolia Sound. When she'd come downstairs this morning for breakfast, however, her mother handed her the house phone because Pops had been calling all day yesterday and all morning.

"Pops, I...I don't know what to say," she admitted, her voice small and trembly. Tears stung her eyes and she hated the whole situation.

Walking away from Jake after everything they'd shared this summer was hard enough –knowing they weren't going to see each other again until next summer was almost unbearable. But to hear him talking to Pops yesterday–especially after he had lied about where he was going to be—something had just snapped in her.

And broke.

Yeah, her heart was definitely broken.

But now she had to consider calling Jake and at least hearing his side of the story. There had been about a dozen calls and texts from him and maybe...just maybe...once she was off the phone with Pops she'd call and they could talk this out.

"Sweet pea, you know I love you," Pops said, interrupting her thoughts, "and I don't want this to come between us."

"It won't, Pops," she promised. "Nothing could ever come between us."

"Okay then," he replied, sounding pleased. "And we'll talk just like we always do and you'll come to visit next summer, right?"

Mallory smiled. "Always. You know I'd never miss a chance to come see you."

"Good. That's good." He paused. "You go and get settled in and visit with your mother and brother and we'll talk soon."

"You know it," she replied softly. "Love you, Pops."

"Love you too."

1

MALLORY THREW her satchel on the sofa as she kicked off her stilettos. It was good to be home. It had been a really long day, but it was a good one though. Great, even! After two years, she was finally getting the promotion she'd been after and a big fat raise to go with it. It felt so good to have all of her hard work recognized and a week from now, she'd have a brand-new office to go with her new executive position.

Of course, that didn't mean she wasn't going to be going out into the field and working on computer systems anymore. It just meant she would be the one overseeing a team and she wouldn't have to be pulling long hours on jobs that were technically beneath her. It was a great feeling.

There had been a cake and champagne to celebrate her new position and her co-workers all congratulated her, but she turned down their offers to go out and continue the celebration. She just wanted to come home and relax for a bit and then call her family to share the good news.

It was after seven and she was starving. The smart thing to do would have been to stop and pick up some takeout on the way home, but getting home was more of a priority. And now what did she have to show for it?

"Ugh...looks like I'm having a sandwich for dinner," she murmured, walking toward her kitchen. "Not exactly the celebratory dinner I should be having." This was becoming the norm lately–not taking enough time for herself and certainly not eating right. "Something's got to give. I can't keep living like this."

Mainly because she wasn't living–she was working long hours, coming home, sleeping, and repeating.

Definitely not the life she wanted to live.

Although, with her promotion, life should get a bit better. Just another few days and it would all kick in. Come Monday morning, there would be light at the end of the tunnel.

Off in the distance, Mallory heard her cellphone ring and sighed. It would be easy to ignore it, but what if it were something important? Making her way back to the living room, she fished her phone out of her purse and smiled when she saw her mother's name on the screen.

"Hey, Mom!"

"Hey, sweetheart! Am I catching you at a bad time?"

"Not at all," she lied. "I was just making some dinner."

"Oh, you're busy."

"No! Really, I'm not, Mom. What's going on? Everything okay?"

The first response was a sigh. "Well...we're having to evacuate."

"What?!" Mallory cried. "When? Why? I thought the hurricane was going to miss you?"

"It's one of those things...it took a turn to the west and

now..." She sighed again. "I'm having a hell of a time with Pops, though. I was hoping you'd talk to him."

Two years ago, Mallory's mother had sold the home on Long Island and moved down to North Carolina's Magnolia Sound to take care of Pops. Susannah Westbrook took her responsibilities and her family seriously and after years of living so far away from her family, she'd finally made the decision to move back to her roots on the Carolina coast.

"Mom, I doubt anything I say will convince him. Surely there's enough people there who can do it. I mean, Aunt Georgia and Uncle Beau can surely talk to him. They've always been the ones to deal with him before, right?"

"In most cases, yes. Believe it or not, he's never evacuated before."

"How is that possible? Parker and Peyton have talked about those evacuations a lot over the years," Mallory argued.

"Well, your cousins–along with your aunt and uncle–always did listen to the warnings and left when they were supposed to. Your great-grandfather, however, has not, and he's refusing to do so now. Honestly, Mal, I don't know what to do. Can you talk to him? Please?"

"Of course I will." Not that it was going to do any good, Mallory already knew this. Her great-grandfather was as stubborn as they came and she knew she could talk and beg and scream and cry until she was blue in the face, but she wasn't going to change his mind. Nothing would. Still, she never turned down an opportunity to talk to him. Not since...

"Hey, sweet pea," Pops said, his voice a little weak and raspy, but that had been something she'd been noticing for some time now.

"Hey, Pops! How are you?"

"How am I? I'm fed up with everyone fussing at me! I've lived in this house for almost a century and no storm has ever forced me out and this one won't either!"

Yup. He was stubborn.

"I know you never had to leave, but...how about just this once you do?" she suggested. "I know it would put everyone's mind at ease and...you know Mom's never gone through a hurricane there. At least, she hasn't in a really long time. She's stressing out about it and I know it would mean a lot if you would go with her."

When he didn't respond right away, Mallory was sure she had him and he was going to agree with her. She was ready to high-five herself when...

"No one's telling her she can't leave," Pops said defiantly. "Heck, it would be a lot easier if she'd go with Georgia and Beau and leave me alone! There's plenty of food here and I have a generator and if I need anything, Jake's right next door!"

Just the mention of Jake Summerford was enough to make Mallory's heart squeeze hard in her chest. It had been six years since they'd had their...what? Affair? Summer fling? Whatever it was, she had ruined it by acting immaturely and Jake hadn't hesitated to remind her of that when she tried to reconcile with him.

She'd given up after three months.

Oh, she'd still gone back to Magnolia Sound to visit Pops and her relatives, but Jake didn't come home at all during his four years of college. The first time she saw him again was two years ago when he came back to work for Coleman Construction. It had been a shock to her system to see him, but it didn't take long for her to realize she had never really meant anything to him. He'd gone back to treating her like nothing more than his neighbor's great-granddaughter.

And it hurt more than anything else ever had in her life.

"...all I'm saying is I'm a grown man who can make his own decisions and I'm tired of everyone treating me like a damn child or some sort of invalid!"

Okay, she'd lost track of the conversation and yet somehow Pops was still carrying on about not evacuating.

"Just...promise me you'll think about it," she quickly interrupted before he went on again. "You know we're all doing this because we love you, so...try not to be so angry, okay?"

"Hmph..."

"Pops..."

"Fine. I'll think about it," he said before quickly adding, "but I'm not going anywhere."

She laughed softly. "I love you, Pops."

"Love you too, sweet pea. When are you coming to visit? We missed you for Fourth of July."

"I know..."

"And you didn't come in June like you said you would..."

Yeah, life had been hectic and she was working with a company who needed a major system overhaul and she couldn't get away, so...

"I'm finishing up with a client next week so I'll look at my calendar and see if I can grab a week to come down. How does that sound?"

"Sounds like you're making excuses, but that's just me," he grumbled.

Okay, so maybe she hadn't wanted to go and visit because whenever she was there, so was Jake. It was like he was more a part of the family than she was and it was just...

awkward. Mallory had considered asking her then-boyfriend Scott if he wanted to go with her for the Fourth of July celebration, but then thought better of it.

Avoidance was way better. The last time she was bold or defiant was that summer with Jake and...

"Here's your mother," Pops said, once again interrupting her thoughts. "Distract her with stories about what's going on with you so she'll leave me alone. Maybe start talking about whatever computer system you're working on. I know I find that stuff hard to follow, I'm sure she will too. And with any luck, she'll forget all about hassling me about leaving my home."

"I'll try," she said with a smile and then he was gone and she could hear him handing the phone back to her mother.

"He's exhausting, Mallory."

"I know, but...you have to see things from his point of view. That house is his whole life. It's his security. Leaving there–even if it's only for a day or two–is going to stress him out a lot."

"It's stressing us all out. Believe me, there's a lot of work that goes into evacuating. We have to secure the house and make sure we have all essential documents along with sorting through everything and just taking the necessities. I'm telling you, I'm a nervous wreck!"

"Is it really bad that he wants to stay?"

"Sweetheart, I understand why he wants to, but at his age, it's just not practical."

"Are you sure no one can stay with him?"

"Jake's offered and I have to tell you, I'm not feeling good about that either."

"Why not?"

"This storm is big. Really big. We're looking at the

possibility of a Category 4 hurricane when it makes land-fall, and basically landfall is…"

"You," Mallory said sadly. "Magnolia Sound is the coast so there is no land before you."

"Exactly," Susannah said. "Georgia and Beau already have a place for us about forty miles inland. It's a town-house they own and rent out but it happens to be vacant so we're all going there. Well…almost all of us are going."

"Mom…I really wish there were something I could do, but…"

"I know, I know. I appreciate you even trying. Georgia was here earlier having a fit and all she managed to do was make things worse. He was almost ready to pack a bag and then she came over and carried on and now he's acting like a petulant child. I tell you, it's maddening!"

"I know Aunt Georgia is not the best in these situations."

"She's not the best in any situation. Honestly, she's almost as obsessed with this house as Pops is! I think that's what got him so worked up again. He accused her of wanting him out of the house so she could somehow try and take it from him!"

"No!" Mallory cried with a small laugh. "I mean I know there's been a lot of heated discussions about her wanting the house, but…how could Pops possibly think that she could use a hurricane evacuation to take it from him?"

"At one point he accused her of being some kind of witch who caused the storm," Susannah said with a hint of amusement. "Look, Georgia is my cousin and I love her, but I swear I want to strangle her sometimes."

"As do her kids," Mallory said with a laugh.

"Oh, that reminds me! Parker's graduation party has been moved to mid-September. I have the date written down here somewhere. Georgia wants to have the party at the country club, but your cousin desperately wants to celebrate someplace fun and a lot less formal. And if I know Parker, she's going to want the kind of party that will make her mother crazy."

"That's reasonable. It's her party, right? But...wait. I didn't realize there was even going to be a party. I thought Parker wanted to go away somewhere rather than have a whole big thing."

"They're doing both, but the vacation is coming first. You know your aunt loves to throw a party, even if it's not the kind of party the guest of honor wants."

That was the truth. Her aunt was the belle of the ball of Magnolia Sound when it came to throwing parties; she lived for occasions to host one. "I'll mark my calendar but text me the date when you find it, please."

"Can do." She sighed. "Okay, I need to go pack up. We're heading out in the morning and there's still so much to do."

"You're just packing up the basics, right?"

"That was the plan, but a bunch of us are helping out the local eateries and getting as much food from them as possible to help cut their losses. Some places closed shop already, but Henderson's Bakery and Café Magnolia put the word out that they had food ready for anyone heading out of town. I'm planning on getting some things for Pops before I go."

"If he loses power, what good will it be?"

"Baked goods will keep," Susannah said. "And I just plan on getting sandwiches from the café that can go in a cooler."

"Where's Gertie? Did she leave already?"

Gertie had been Pops' housekeeper for longer than

Mallory was alive. She was practically family. "She was out of town visiting her family and when the news first mentioned the storm, we told her to stay put."

"That was smart of you, but I'm sure she's worried."

"She only comes in once a week now," Susannah said. "I think she's ready to retire but she doesn't want to leave Pops."

That sounded like Gertie, all right.

"Okay, sweetie, I'll call you once we're settled."

"Be safe, Mom. And please keep talking to Pops. Maybe have...have Jake talk to him. I'm sure he'd listen to him before anyone else."

"Hmm...you may be right. I'll do that. Have a good night, sweetheart."

"You too, Mom. I'll talk to you tomorrow."

Once they hung up, Mallory's stomach growled loudly and she went back to the kitchen to make herself a sandwich. She didn't have much to choose from and ended up with ham and swiss on whole wheat. Not the most inspired dinner, but with her plate in hand, she went back to the sofa and turned on the TV, hoping to catch the weather report.

_____

"And now the latest on the storm that has the mid-Atlantic coast holding its breath. Hurricane Amelia has picked up strength as she seems to be heading directly toward the Carolinas. With the projected path, the storm should make landfall late Thursday night. The first evacuation orders have been issued to all coastal residents up and down the Carolina coast, with mandatory evacuation orders expected to go out within the next twelve hours. Residents on the barrier islands, Outer Banks, and Magnolia

Sound areas in North Carolina look to be in the direct path of Amelia. Right now, this is a Category 2 hurricane, but predictions have it hitting Category 3 after midnight tonight with the possibility of hitting Category 4 by the time it makes landfall. And we all know when winds range from 131 to 155 mph, they can cause catastrophic damage to property, humans, and animals. Severe structural damage to frame homes, apartments, and shopping centers should be expected. Category 4 hurricanes often include long-term power outages and water shortages lasting from a few weeks to a few months, so again, it's important for any remaining residents to have a significant nonperishable food and water supply at hand."

Her appetite gone, Mallory tossed her sandwich back onto the plate and grabbed the remote to change the channel. There wasn't anything she could do from here–last she checked not only was Garden City, New York still eleven hours from Magnolia Sound, but she also had zero ability to stop a hurricane.

"Oh, but if I could," she murmured, standing and taking her sad dinner back to the kitchen and tossing it into the trash. "Now what do I do?"

Unfortunately, her first thought was to reach out to Jake and beg him to convince Pops to leave in the morning with everyone. It would be a completely legitimate reason for calling, but...

"Screw it. I don't care about how I feel or how Jake may feel about me calling. This isn't about us, so...if he doesn't like it, too bad."

Sometimes you had to put your own feelings aside and do the uncomfortable things–the things that make your heart ache and make you feel like you're going to be sick. And as she scrolled through her phone and pulled up his number, she was seriously glad she didn't take more than a couple of bites of her sandwich because...

"Hello?"

Just the sound of his voice was enough to make her want to pass out.

Very few things in life took Jake Summerford for surprise.

Mallory Westbrook was one of them.

Seeing her name appear on his phone filled him with a myriad of emotions, but he knew if she was calling him, something serious had to be going on. She hadn't willingly called him in over five years.

"Hey, Jake," she said softly and he could hear the tremble in her voice, could almost picture her fidgeting with her hair.

"What's up, Mal?" He hoped she'd get right to the point. With this storm coming in, he had a lot to do. The only reason he was home and willing to answer a call was because he'd stopped boarding up the house so he could come inside and grab something to eat. He looked down at the sandwich he'd made and opted to take a bite while she talked.

"Um, I'm sorry to bother you – I'm sure you're busy with this storm coming in - but I just got off the phone with my mom and she said Pops is refusing to evacuate."

He swallowed his bite and nodded. "Yeah, I was over there earlier and he's pretty much dug his heels in on this."

"He can't stay there, Jake! You have to convince him to leave!"

Tossing the sandwich down, he began to pace. "What would you like me to do, Mal?" he snapped. "No one can force him to leave and I'm not about to physically remove him from his home!" He heard her soft sob on the other end of the line and cursed. "Look, he has a storm shelter and we both know in all the years he's lived here, storm damage has been minimal. I think the forecasters are being a little overzealous about the storm. He has plenty of supplies and even if he loses power, that's nothing for old Zeke, you know that."

"He's too old to ride out a storm on his own," she argued, but there was very little heat behind her words. "I know he's stubborn and I know he thinks he's invincible, but..."

"Yeah, I know," he said, going to sit down on his sofa.

"Mom just called and put me on the phone with him and he's not thinking clearly," she went on. "He's being defiant because of Aunt Georgia – at least, that's part of it. But someone needs to make him see some sense here, Jake!"

"In his mind, he IS seeing sense! Hell, he's lived a long time and has survived many a storm here! And on top of that, he hates how everyone is constantly trying to tell him how to live and treating him like he's a child!"

"No one's trying to treat him like he's a child! That's ridiculous! We're all just concerned for his safety! Can't you get the sheriff or someone from the local police to come and make him leave?"

He swiped a weary hand over his face. "You're kidding, right?"

"Not even a little," she said stiffly, and Jake knew how much she hated to feel like she wasn't being taken seriously.

"Mal, they're a little busy right now with securing the entire damn community. I greatly doubt they have time to convince one resident to leave."

"He's a founding member of Magnolia Sound! Doesn't that count for anything?" she cried with frustration.

"I don't really see how that's relevant right now to anybody," he said, feeling frustrated enough himself. "It's not like they're going to go around town and check on people in the order of some ridiculous list of who's more important. That's just crazy."

She was silent for a long moment and Jake knew she was simply trying to come up with a clever retort. There was a time when he used to enjoy this kind of banter–some of their biggest arguments had led to the hottest sex.

Well, that's not going to happen right now no matter how big the argument...

True enough, but his mind still went there.

"So you're not going to help? Is that it?"

"Mallory, I was over there already and talked to him. What more do you want me to do?" he demanded.

"Protect him! After everything he's done for you..." But she stopped before saying anything else and he wasn't sure if he was relieved or pissed off by it.

Raking a hand through his hair, he sighed loudly. "I'm boarding up my place now and I had a crew over at Zeke's doing the same earlier. Everyone's heading out either tonight or tomorrow morning, but...I can stay with him."

Her soft gasp affected him more than it should.

"You...you would do that?"

"I talked to your mom about it and she's not thrilled at that even being an option, but I don't see any others. At least if I'm there with him we'll know he'll be okay and I'll be able to take care of any situation that may come up with debris or damage to the house." He paused and realized how cocky that sounded. "I mean, I can assess the damage and do my best to keep him out of harm's way so he doesn't try to tackle anything on his own."

"Jake, I...it's not safe for either of you. Maybe if you tell him you don't think it's safe to stay, he'll leave."

"Already tried. I'm telling you, I've never seen him more adamant. Something about this storm has him all riled up."

And it was frustrating as hell because really, Jake had every intention of evacuating with the masses as soon as he secured his house. It was his childhood home and when his parents decided to retire and move to Arizona two years ago, Jake knew he didn't want another family living in it. So he'd bought it from them. They'd argued about it and eventually agreed but only after putting a ridiculously low price tag on it. He knew the place was worth so much more, but they knew what amount they needed to help them relocate. And the bottom line was they wanted to do something for him that they hadn't been able to most of his life.

Now he was a homeowner in the town he loved more than anything and there was a chance the entire thing was going to get destroyed in a massive, once-in-a-lifetime kind of storm. He wanted to howl at the unfairness of it all, but... when had his life ever been easy?

"So there's really nothing we can do?" she asked sadly, and more than anything Jake wished he could reassure her—give her hope. But he couldn't.

"I'll try again, but...I can't make any promises."

They were silent for a long moment and honestly, he didn't know what to say.

Liar. Ask her how she is, how her job is, when is she coming back to Magnolia Sound so you can just see her and know she's all right...

"I should go," he said instead. "I've got a lot to get done before morning, so..."

"Oh, okay," she said, her voice quiet. "Um...thanks for taking the time to talk to me and for looking after Pops."

"It's not a problem." He paused and when she didn't speak again, he said, "Take care, Mal."

"You too, Jake. And please...be safe."

And then she was gone and Jake felt all the air rush out of his lungs. Tossing the phone aside, he closed his eyes and wondered when things would change. When would there come a time when just the sound of Mallory's voice didn't make him wish for things he couldn't have?

They were over. Ancient history. And when he looked back, he knew it was for the best. At that point in their lives they were going in completely opposite directions and Mallory had proven that she still needed to grow up.

And she has...

Oh, man, the last time she was back in Magnolia Sound–which was a year ago–he had been shocked at the changes in her. She was still beautiful–maybe even more so–but she carried herself with such grace and elegance that made her even more attractive. Everything in him had reacted to her in such a powerful way that he left town for most of her visit just so he wouldn't be tempted to seek her out.

It was the sight of her standing out on the dock next to the boathouse that had done him in. Late one afternoon, he had been walking over to talk to Zeke when he spotted Mallory down by the water. She'd been in a long, flowing dress and there was a soft breeze that had the material molded to one side. It had reminded him of all the days and nights they had spent down there together. One look and it had taken every ounce of will he had not to go down to her because he knew if he did, he would have kissed her and begged her to go into the boathouse like they used to and make love to her all night long. He fought to remember how things had ended–how she ran and refused to listen, how she cried and apologized, and how he had been the one to say it was all too much.

And it was.

She was a distraction and his life was at a point where he needed total focus. Naturally she hadn't taken his rejection well and when she was on the verge of wearing him down–of convincing him they could still make things work– he had done something he swore he'd never do.

He lied.

Looking back, he knew it was a mistake to go that route, but at the time he had needed to make a clean break so he could get his head in the game with college. Taking a six-year break between high school and college hadn't been part of his plan, but that's the way things had worked out and once he finally had his opportunity, he wasn't going to blow it by distracting himself with a long-distance relationship. It seemed logical back then, but right now? Not so much. If he could go back in time…

But he couldn't and it was pointless to even go there or think about it.

Outside the wind was whipping and he could already hear some branches of nearby trees banging against the house. Time to stop walking down memory lane and get back to what was important–securing his and Zeke's homes and doing what he could to convince his neighbor to evacuate.

Spotting his sandwich, Jake walked over and quickly wolfed it down, then grabbed a bottle of water and took a long drink. It was going to be a long night and he needed to keep his strength up if he was going to get everything he needed to done. Grabbing his tablet, he pulled up his to-do list and scanned it.

"Board up the windows, check. Secure the outside furniture and put what I can in storage, check." Walking to his pantry, he checked on his emergency supplies. "Batteries, radio, water, candles, first aid kit, canned goods...check."

Next he walked into his bedroom and double checked all the documents he had placed in the safe earlier–insurance policies, photos, birth certificate–it seemed crazy, but the safe was water and fireproof. He knew that if anything should happen to the house, the important stuff should be safe.

Walking through the house, he felt restless. In the last two years he had done renovations on the place and updated so many things. The thought of it all going to waste in a storm made his stomach churn. This was one of the sad realities of living on the coast and it was something he'd lived with his entire life, but it was the first time it was happening to him as an adult, where it was a place that was totally his.

"Don't think about it," he warned himself. "There's a good chance this storm will turn or weaken in the next twenty-four hours. Think positively."

That was easier said than done when he could hear the wind from inside the house. Turning around, he grabbed his rain gear and put it back on before grabbing his phone and slipping it into his pocket. With a steadying breath, he walked outside and went back to work securing the two properties as best as he could.

2

Mallory sat glued to her television for the next two days, calling in sick because she wasn't going to be able to focus on anything anyway. It wasn't a total loss because there was still so much she could do remotely, so she set up her laptop on her coffee table and did as much work as she could while keeping the Weather Channel on non-stop.

With each update, her optimism that the storm might weaken shrunk. It wasn't going to downgrade to a Category 1 and it wasn't going to turn and head out into the Atlantic. Every hour, her anxiety level grew. She had checked in every hour with her mother and as of noon, everyone was at Aunt Georgia and Uncle Beau's townhouse.

Except Pops.

She cried when her mother called this morning and told her how she left the big coastal plantation home and waved goodbye to Pops and Jake as she pulled away. Then they'd both cried for several minutes without speaking. Her heart hurt so much and it felt like she was right there in the car with her mother. Mallory could clearly see Jake and Pops on the grand front porch waving goodbye.

After that, she had tried to call Pops, but the call never went through. Then she had tried to call Jake and it went directly to voicemail.

Not the most encouraging sign...

Right on cue, her phone rang and she knew without even looking that it was her mother. Grabbing the remote, she muted the television before answering. "Hey," she said breathlessly. "Any updates? Has anyone talked to Pops?"

Susannah sighed. "Not directly, but I did get a call from Colton Hale a little while ago and he stopped by the house on his way out of town. He said that other than some downed branches, everything looked good and both Pops and Jake were fine."

"Wait...who's Colton Hale?"

"He's one of the foremen who works for Coleman. He's done some work on the house for us and he was part of the crew Jake sent over yesterday to help board everything up."

"Oh. That was nice of him to stop by and check on things," Mallory said, feeling at least a little relief at knowing someone had actually gone and seen them for themselves. "So...now what? I've tried calling both Pops and Jake and my calls aren't going through. I hate how they're cut off from everyone."

"I know it's not ideal but cell service is spotty at best right now. Colton said he had tried to call me several times before it actually went through."

"It's nice that he kept trying." She paused. "What are all of you going to do? I mean I know you're at the townhouse and all, but the storm's still going to hit that area too."

"Now we just have to sit and wait, unfortunately. They're not letting anyone back over the bridge so even if we wanted to go back, we can't. The evacuation route has all lanes going in a single direction–away from the coast–so for now we can only sit and watch it all unfold on the television." She paused and then groaned.

"What? What's the matter?"

"The power's already flickering. So basically we can only sit and watch it unfold until we lose power."

"Oh, Mom...I wish there was something I could do."

"Me too. I'm just glad you're safe and not having to deal with this. It's hard enough worrying about everyone here."

"At least you're not all crammed in there. I'm guessing Mason, Parker, and Peyton aren't there with you, are they?"

Susannah chuckled softly. "Mason's here because he was told to come and help, but Parker went with Tyler to Raleigh for the weekend. That's where his family is now. And Peyton was already on vacation out in L.A. and decided to extend it until the storm passed."

"Lucky her," Mallory murmured. "So now you're stuck all weekend with Mason the Magnificent?"

Still laughing, her mother gently chided her. "That's not nice, Mallory. And really, I would think he's outgrown that nickname–no matter what your brother says."

"Speaking of Sam, have you heard from him lately?"

"Other than a quick call to make sure I'm all right? No."

Her twin brother made her crazier than anyone else possibly could. Always the hellraiser of the family, he'd become harder and harder to pin down in the last couple of years. He was living in Virginia now, but no one saw much of him and he wasn't particularly forthcoming with what was going on in his life.

Although...Mallory managed to get at least two calls a month from him and even though most of the time they talked about her, it made her feel better just hearing his voice.

"I don't think the storm's supposed to reach him, is it?" she asked.

"He's about two hours inland so the most he'll probably see is tropical storm levels of rain," her mother replied. "When he called, he mentioned heading to the mountains this weekend to see some friends so, who knows? Maybe he personally won't be affected by the storm at all."

"Typical Sam. He always does seem to escape before things get rough." And although it didn't particularly sound like a loving comment, it really was. Her brother had a knack for wreaking havoc no matter where he went, but there were never any consequences. It was like some sort of gift he had–always managing to escape bad situations unscathed.

There was some static on the line and it didn't take long for either of them to realize they were losing their connection. "I'll either call or text you later and let you know what's going on, Mal. I love you!"

"Love you too, Mom!" And when they hung up, Mallory reached for the remote and turned the volume back on so she could hear the updates.

For hours, nothing changed. The only updates on-screen were the images and, considering the size of the storm, it wasn't only Magnolia Sound that was getting hit. Mallory sat patiently and tried to work and not obsess about things she couldn't change, but...

Grabbing her phone, she tried to call Pops again and unfortunately had the same results. It was maddening. She received texts from her mother and other than sitting back and accepting the fact that there was nothing she could do, well...there was literally nothing she could do other than work.

Which sucked because her eyes couldn't seem to focus

on the reports she was reading and the last thing on her mind was computer system optimization.

Closing the laptop, Mallory stood and stretched, then called in an order for Chinese takeout. "No sandwich for me tonight," she said, feeling proud of herself for remembering that she needed to eat. And as she sat back down on the couch, that opened a whole other can of worms for her.

Her life.

What was she doing with her life? It was work, work, and more work. Her social life was almost as non-existent as her sex life. Sure there had been Mark, but that lasted less than a month and they'd never gotten to the bedroom.

Not for lack of trying on his part, but lack of enthusiasm on hers. He was a nice enough guy and they both worked in the same field and had a lot to talk about, but there wasn't anything about him that got her excited or even remotely thinking sexy thoughts of him.

Yeah, something had to give. Soon. This was so not her dream life. Sure, things were beginning to look up at work and she was really excited about this new position, but she was tired of being alone–missed being in a relationship and having some companionship.

And she really missed sex.

With a weary sigh, she let her head rest back against the cushions. What else could she possibly do? She took her job seriously and had a strong work ethic. It wasn't a crime, right? But it certainly didn't leave a lot of time for a social life. Hopefully that would change, but...even if she suddenly had an abundance of time on her hands, how was she supposed to go about meeting people again? Dating apps? Bars? Joining a sports league or something? Or maybe...something along the lines of finding a hobby?

A hobby!

Sitting up, she felt the first twinges of excitement. A hobby would be the absolute perfect thing to keep her from spending her free time reading technical magazines and reports and meeting new people! But what did she want to do...

Her mind immediately went to the work she had done on the boathouse at Pops' place. Doing the decorating had been something she enjoyed so much and as she looked around her condo, Mallory smiled at what she created there as well. Decorating certainly wasn't a hobby–after all, how many times could she possibly re-do her own place?–and it wouldn't particularly lead to meeting eligible men.

"Okay, scratch that idea," she muttered, then looked over at the color on the opposite wall and thought about maybe re-doing that, at least. "Great, there's four hours of my time to play around with."

Ugh...it shouldn't be this hard, she thought. People had hobbies, right? She had friends who did crafty things like scrapbooking and painting, and then there were more of the activity variety like yoga or Zumba...maybe she should join a gym! That was also a great place to meet single guys and make new friends!

Her excitement lasted all of one minute before the thought of it exhausted her. She'd have to remember to bring a gym bag and a change of clothes to work every day. Then she remembered how out of shape she was and worried she'd make a fool out of herself and fall off a tread-mill or something. Plus, at the end of a long work day, the last thing she was going to want to do was work out and get sweaty.

And...scratch another idea.

Glancing at the clock, Mallory saw she still had another twenty minutes before her food would arrive. She didn't want to open her computer and work, and she didn't want to simply sit and stare at the TV and listen to more bad news.

When her cellphone rang, she let out a loud scream. Sam's name came up on the screen and she instantly relaxed. Swiping the screen, she said, "And you say twin telepathy isn't a thing!"

"Huh? What are you talking about?"

"I was just sitting here trying to think of something to do and then here you are–calling me!" She curled up on the sofa, tucking her feet under her to get comfortable. "So how are you?"

Chuckling, he replied, "You're so damn weird, but yeah, you were on my mind and I figured I'd give you a call while I was driving. What's going on?"

"I'm sitting here freaking out while watching the news."

"Then turn off the TV, dork," he said, still laughing.

"Sam..."

"Yeah, yeah, yeah, I get it. This storm is bad and you're worried about everyone, but Mom says it's all under control. She's at Aunt Georgia's place and other than the power flickering, they're all okay. What's freaking you out?"

"They're not all okay, you idiot!" she cried. "Pops refused to leave! So he's at home and probably has no power by now and I hate it! Just the thought of it makes me want to cry!"

"Oh, right. Yeah, she told me about that, but you know Pops, Mal. He's as tough as they come and storms like this don't freak him out."

"That's just the thing, Sam. Magnolia Sound has never had a storm like this! He has no idea what he's in for and I can't believe no one would force him to leave!"

"He's not completely alone. Jake's there with him..."

She groaned. "Great. So if something happens, they'll both be in danger. Way to make me feel better, Sam."

He let out a long breath. "What do you want me to say, Mal?" he said irritably. "I get it. You're worried. We all are. But there's nothing we can do but hope they're going to be all right, so...let's talk about something else, okay?"

"Fine," she grumbled, knowing her brother was right. It was a vicious cycle to keep obsessing about the storm and her family's safety. "Who are you going to visit in the mountains?"

"How'd you know about that?"

"Mom told me."

"Oh. One of the guys I work with has a cabin and we're going to do some fishing. We figured it was better to get away for the weekend than to sit here and deal with this weather. There's about five of us going so...you know...guys' weekend."

"Nice. Maybe I should look into planning a girls' weekend."

A snort of laughter came out before he spoke. "Right. Like you'd take time off for something so frivolous."

"What's that supposed to mean?" she demanded.

"It means you are a bit of an obsessive workaholic. The only time you take time off is when we have some sort of family thing down by Pops. So while I think it's adorable that you're even mentioning a girls' weekend, we both know it's never going to happen. Unless you're counting hanging out with Parker and Peyton while you're already visiting with everyone."

Dammit, she hated when he had a point.

"Fine, so I don't do a lot of that kind of thing. So what? It's not like your fishing weekend is the most exciting thing in the world!"

Gah! Could I sound any pettier?

"You're so competitive, Mal. Unclench a bit," Sam said reasonably. "How's work going?"

"Actually...I got a promotion! Effective this coming Monday!"

"Wow! Congratulations! So what is it that you do? Build computers or something, right?"

She sighed. It didn't matter how many times she described her job to him; Sam never seemed to get it. So rather than explain it again, she simply replied, "Not exactly. It's just...you know...all boring tech stuff."

"And why did you opt to go into that field again? Because I have to tell you, you have never sounded enthused about your career. Ever."

"Oh, and you do?" she replied sarcastically.

"Clearly you're in a pissy mood and I shouldn't have called..."

"No, no, no...you're right. I'm sorry. I really am being a brat." She groaned. "I'm glad you're going away for the weekend. And...I'm jealous."

Mallory could practically feel him grinning triumphantly.

"Now, that wasn't so hard, was it?"

She laughed. "Yes, it was!"

"Yeah, but you'll survive. So what else is going on with you? Anything?"

"I was trying to come up with a hobby. Turns out I don't have one."

"Hmm...that's...wow. Sad but true. You really don't have a hobby. You should seriously get one."

"That's what I was just trying to figure out. I don't even know what I like to do other than decorating and that's not really a hobby. It's more like a career."

"So change careers!" Sam said with the same exuberance he gave to everything.

She envied that about him.

"Sam, you don't just go and change careers! I've invested a lot of time, money, and energy into what I do! And I happen to enjoy it!"

"Do you? Because it never seems that way. And I change careers all the time! It's not possible to simply go to college, pick a career, and never do anything else for the rest of your life. It just isn't," he explained levelly. "How do you know there isn't anything else out there for you? Or something you may like even better? Remember the summer you did all that work on the boathouse? You loved it! We all thought you'd go into decorating."

Yeah, she had loved it and in a perfect world it would have been a career path for her, but...she lacked the confidence to try. What she was doing now was a good, solid career choice. If she stayed up-to-date with technology, she would always have a job. If she did something different like decorating, though...

"I can hear you thinking from here, Mal."

"I just don't think I'm the kind of person who can just... switch careers. It seems like a huge risk. And with this new promotion..."

"Fine, don't change careers," he said with a small sigh. "But you really do need to do something about a hobby. And a social life."

If only it were that easy...

"I don't even know where to begin," she admitted. "I never gave it much thought. Computers and technology have been my only interests for a while now."

"I don't know what to tell you, Mal. You're just going to have to get out there and find some new interests."

They were talking in circles and weren't getting anywhere. Changing the subject was the only way to keep her sane. "So tell me about this cabin!"

"Can I let you in on a little secret?"

"Sure."

"I keep a couple of bottles of whiskey down here that no one knows about," Zeke said with an impish grin. "Gertie would have my hide if she knew I was still having a shot a day. Hell, Susannah would too."

Jake couldn't help but laugh. The power was out, they were down in the storm cellar, and truth be told, he was more than a little scared. The wind was like nothing he ever seen. Magnolia Sound had risen so much that most of Zeke's yard was flooded, and at last check, they'd lost about a dozen trees. Luckily the house was up on a hill so they were somewhat safe, but in his entire life, he'd never witnessed a hurricane like this and he prayed he never would again.

Then said another prayer he'd live through this one.

"How did you manage to keep it from Gertie? She rules this place with a bit of an iron first." The truth was, Gertie was almost seventy now and she was more like family than hired help. Jake had a feeling she knew more than she let on, but also knew when to simply let something slide.

Zeke waved him off. "She likes to think she runs this place, but there's plenty I don't tell her and she doesn't know."

Again, Jake doubted it, but he'd humor Zeke.

It was a good way to pass the time.

It was only seven o'clock but it was already dark out and

they had no power. They were using one of the battery-powered lanterns to see each other. They'd played several games of poker, listened to the radio for weather updates, and ate a couple of sandwiches for dinner. Undoubtedly, Zeke would be asleep within the hour and then Jake would be alone with his thoughts–too keyed up to sleep.

"I used to keep cigars down here, but the damn things smell enough that Gertie caught me," Zeke said with a small laugh. "I know she's just looking out for me, but at my age, I should be able to enjoy the things I want without anyone giving me any grief." He paused and leaned back in his chair, a piece of lawn furniture they'd pulled inside for safe-keeping. "No one lives forever, Jake. No amount of good, clean living is going to change that. Trust me."

Unsure of what to say, Jake simply nodded.

"I've lived longer than anyone in my family," Zeke went on. "I'm ninety-six years old. My father died when he was sixty. My mother lived to be eighty." He paused. "I outlived my wife and children." He paused again and wiped at his eyes before looking at Jake again. "I'm tired, son. I've lived a good life. And if I want to sit here and have some whiskey and smoke a cigar...well...I should be able to."

Then he slowly stood up and walked over to the row of shelves in the far corner. Jake figured he was going to grab the whiskey. He could use a shot of it himself. This was all a lot harder on his nerves than he thought it would be. There wasn't any reception for his cell phone and he wished more than anything that he could talk to someone and let them know they were okay. None of his texts were going through, but that didn't mean he'd stop trying. At some point they would but right now he just wished he could connect with the outside world.

Zeke came back and sat down, placing a bottle of Johnnie Walker Double Black on the table along with two shot glasses and two cigars. The smile on the old man's face was one of pure glee.

Shaking his head, Jake smiled too.

"The last two," Zeke said with a wink.

Doing his best to sit back, relax, and ignore the harsh sounds of Mother Nature just outside the door, Jake accepted the shot glass. "What are we drinking to?"

Maybe it was the lighting or maybe it was just his imagination, but for a second he swore Zeke's expression went sad. But in the blink of an eye, he was smiling again. "To life," he said with a bit of gusto. "To life with a good woman." He paused. "And I had the best. Can't wait to see her again." He touched his glass to Jake's. "Cheers!"

The liquor burned going down but right now, he welcomed it. Placing his glass back on the table, he laughed softly when Zeke handed him a cigar. Smoking was never his thing, but he figured right now, why not?

They sat in companionable silence, each lost in their own thoughts as they lit their cigars. It took a lot of effort not to cough, but it wasn't nearly as unpleasant as Jake thought it would be.

"Can I ask you something?" Zeke asked, his voice a little softer than it had been a minute ago.

"Sure."

"You gonna stay here in Magnolia Sound?"

He nodded. "That's the plan." Then he waited for Zeke to expand on that question, but he didn't. Instead, he gave Jake a curt nod and went back to his cigar.

The silence continued for a few more minutes before Zeke spoke again. "You want to know something funny?"

It was obvious his old friend's train of thought was all over the place tonight, and Jake knew he'd go on humoring him as long as he needed to. "Sure."

"I always wished all the kids–the grandkids and great-grandkids–would move back here someday. There's something that does my heart good when I see them all here." He let out a long breath and took another puff of his cigar. "Holidays and birthdays are all a great excuse to get together, but I fear everyone will continue to spread out all over the damn place and soon no one will remember that a family founded this town." He paused. "Because that family is gone."

Damn. "You know that's never going to happen, Zeke. Georgia and Beau are never going to leave Magnolia and you know they won't let Mason leave either," he added with a slight chuckle. "Parker and Peyton are always going to come back here because of their parents."

"Hmph...maybe."

"Susannah came back," Jake went on. "And you know she's been gone the longest."

"She only came back to take care of me because Georgia wanted to put me in a home and take my house for herself," he groused. "Well, she's in for a rude awakening."

Jake knew better than to touch that comment with a ten-foot pole.

"I know it's been a while since Cash has been home, but you know Grace and the boys have always been nearby. They're here for every holiday and every occasion."

"It's not the same as them being part of the town. But I will say this, those three boys are hell-raisers and maybe it's a good thing they didn't live here when they were younger. They're turning into grown men now. It's time they act more responsibly."

Jake nodded but didn't want to comment. There was no doubt that Garrett, Jackson, and Austin Coleman were handfuls. The stories about their antics always abounded at Coleman family gatherings. But Zeke had a point–it was definitely a benefit that they weren't pulling pranks here in Magnolia Sound. Poor Zeke would have lost his mind trying to deal with them over the years.

"Back when I was younger, we all had a hand in this town. I still do," he stated. "No one pays much attention to it, but I still own a dozen businesses here. Why? Because it's important for me to stay involved. I like the connection to my community. I don't understand why it's not something this younger generation wants."

"Different times, Zeke. It's a different world than when you were growing up."

"Don't I know it." He paused and took another puff of his cigar. "I'd like to think I left a good legacy for the great-grandkids and that they appreciate it."

"Zeke..."

The old man looked at him, his expression somewhat fierce. "This town is going to be a mess after this storm does its damage. Everyone's going to look around and be sad because so much will be gone." He paused. "But I want them to look around and be thankful for all that remains."

Before Jake could ask what that meant, Zeke was standing and stretching before putting out his cigar. "As much as I'd like to stay up and see what Mother Nature has in store for us, it's past my bedtime." He gave a small wave and turned toward the back of the cellar where the cots were. He'd only gone a few steps when he turned around. "You're a good man, Jacob. You've always been like one of my great-grandkids and I'm thankful you cared enough to stay. Not just here in Magnolia, but here today with me."

And damn if that didn't choke him up a bit. Putting out his cigar, Jake stood and walked over to Zeke. Placing a hand on his long-time mentor's shoulder, he said, "There was no way I was leaving you here alone. We're in this together."

Nodding, Zeke motioned toward the cots. "They're not the most comfortable things, but I've slept on worse. Make sure to try and get some sleep."

"I will."

Zeke studied him for a long moment and Jake was certain there was more he wanted to say. But al he said was "Good night."

Jake took a step back and watched as Zeke settled in and turned out the lantern that was back there. He contemplated trying to catch a couple of hours of sleep himself, but his mind wasn't ready to shut down yet. Walking back over toward the door to the cellar, he opted to go out and check on the upstairs to make sure things were still intact.

It didn't take long to see that so far there were no obvious signs of damage to the house and no leaks that he could find. Of course the worst of the storm had yet to hit and they still had another twenty-four hours to get through before they could say the worst was behind them.

Back on the lower level of the house was the lone door they hadn't covered with boards and Jake braced himself as he stepped outside. There a deck above him that offered some protection from the rain and it felt good to breathe in some fresh air. After a few minutes, he knew he had to go back inside because the wind and rain were just too much to take.

After an hour, he gave up the fight and figured he'd try to get some sleep. After tossing and turning and trying to get comfortable, Jake realized Zeke was right—the cots weren't very comfortable—but once he accepted that fact and cleared his mind, he did fall asleep.

There was a loud crash in the distance and Jake woke up instantly. He had no idea how long he had been asleep—was it minutes? Hours? —but he jumped up from the cot and immediately went in search of what had happened.

Out of the cellar, he walked up the stairs to the main floor of the house and felt a definite breeze coming from somewhere. Pulling his phone from his pocket, he also saw it was almost five in the morning and was surprised he had slept all night. Moving from room to room, he noted the kitchen, dining room, and living room were all in good condition. Moving to the other side of the house, he saw that Zeke's office was fine as well. Down the hall he went to the newer wing of the house. It was where there were two guest rooms and Zeke's suite.

"Damn," he muttered, seeing that a tree had crushed the front corner of the house and one of the guest rooms was completely destroyed. He hated that it happened but was relieved it was this side of the house and not the original structure. Closing the door to that room seemed like the only thing he could do to keep the elements at least partially at bay.

Moving across the hall to Zeke's room, he paused. Why was the door closed? When he had walked around last night, he knew all the doors were opened. Shaking his head, he opened the door and froze.

Zeke was in the bed.

"You stubborn little rascal," he whispered, softly chuckling to himself. It shouldn't have surprised him. It was amazing he had kept Zeke down in the cellar as long as he had. And he said a quick prayer of thanks the tree hadn't made it to this side of the house.

Then something else occurred to him.

Why wasn't Zeke awake?

The noise of the tree crashing on the house was loud enough that it woke Jake up, and he was on the other side of the house, a floor down, in a highly-insulated cellar. How could Zeke sleep through that? How could...?

"No," he said in a near sob. His entire body began to tremble and he quickly walked over next to the bed. Jake reached out and touched Zeke's shoulder. It was all he had to do. Dropping to his knees, he put his head on the mattress and cried like he hadn't in years.

Maybe ever.

When he looked up, he saw how peaceful his friend looked and thought about all the things they'd talked about the night before.

This was why Zeke didn't want to leave.

He knew it was his time and wanted to be here in his own home, his own bed.

And damn if that didn't make him start crying again.

How was he supposed to tell Zeke's family? How was he supposed to break the news to everyone in this town that the man who meant so much to so many was gone?

Zeke's words from the previous night came to mind and he realized how prophetic they actually were. *Soon no one will remember that a family founded this town. Because that family is gone.*

"I'll never let that happen," he said quietly, his voice trembling. "No one will ever forget you or all that you've done for this town. You touched so many lives and I promise that your legacy will live on." His throat clogged with emotion as an entire lifetime of memories seemed to play out in his mind. Old Zeke had been there for every milestone in Jake's life – there wasn't a time when he hadn't been there with praise or encouragement or even some stern advice. How was he supposed to move forward without him? How was anyone who knew him?

He had no idea how much time he stayed there kneeling beside the bed with one hand on Zeke's shoulder. Again, it could have been minutes or even hours. But before he moved, he had some things he needed to say.

"You're the reason I am who I am today," he said, his voice cracking slightly. "You took a chance on me when I was just a kid and taught me more than anyone else I've ever met. Hell, I wouldn't be the man I am today if it wasn't for you. You know I love my parents and they are amazing, but you always understood me in a way they never did." He paused. "Last night you said you always thought of me as one of your great-grandkids, and I want you to know...what I should have told you...is that I've always thought of you as not just my grandfather, but one of my best friends and a mentor. You meant the world to me, Zeke. The world is going to be a much lonelier place without you." Another pause. "I can only hope that I make you proud. That I live up to everything you saw in me."

Standing, he took another minute to compose himself. "Thank you for letting me be a part of your family. I promise to make sure no one in this town forgets you." He gave a trembly smile. "And I hope you're finally sitting and holding hands with that beautiful wife of yours. I bet she was glad to finally see you and welcome you home."

Then, slowly and reverently, he pulled the sheet up and covered his friend before walking out of the room.

Outside the weather was angry and Jake wanted to howl with the wind and let out his own anger and devastation over this cruel twist of fate. As he made his way back toward the living room, he knew nothing was ever going to be the same again—not the town, not the family, but most of all, him.

3

MALLORY STOOD at the curb outside of baggage claim and willed herself not to cry. It had been a losing battle for more than three days, so she had no idea why she thought it would work now. Looking to her left, she spotted her mother's car. Picking up her luggage, she made her way through the small crowd of people and waited for her mother to pull up.

At the curb, Susannah stopped and parked before getting out to help Mallory with the bags. Once they were situated in the trunk, she turned and hugged her daughter. They clung to each other even as they cried. Several horns sounded at them, and within minutes they were in the car and pulling away.

"How was your flight?"

Shrugging, Mallory said, "Uneventful. No delays or screaming babies. That's a win in my book."

They both laughed softly before Susannah spoke. "I was surprised you wanted to fly. You normally enjoy the drive."

"Under any other circumstance I do, but...I just felt like

I needed to get here. Not that flying saved a lot of time. Between arriving at the airport early, changing flights in Charlotte..."

"It still saved you about four and a half hours, though. That's not a bad thing."

"True." She sighed and looked out at the passing scenery. Everything was gray and wet and it all looked... normal. "Have you been back to the house yet?"

Her mother glanced at her briefly. "This morning," she replied before letting out her own long breath. "It was...it was hard, Mallory, and you need to be prepared."

She felt her body begin to tremble and all she could do was nod.

"The front corner of the house is crushed. The large magnolia tree in the front yard lost its longest limb. That's what hit the house." She paused. "The back deck is gone– another casualty of the massive tree limbs in the yard. The pier lost a few boards, but for the most part it's intact, as is the boathouse – which surprised us all because the Sound had flooded."

"Pops built things to last," she said quietly.

"That he did."

She nodded again. "What about the rest of the town?"

"It's a mess. I didn't go too far into downtown, but Georgia called when she got home and told me it looked utterly devastated as she drove through. There are so many trees down and there's flooding...it just breaks my heart."

"Is there power yet?"

"Not yet, but we were told we'd have it back by tomorrow."

"Where are we staying?"

"Remarkably, Georgia and Beau's house didn't sustain any major damage. They have downed trees, but nothing hit the house, thankfully. Beau and Mason took all the boards down from the doors and windows and they've got a generator and said we can stay with them. Of course, if you'd prefer, we can stay at their townhouse too. You know, in case you want power and air conditioning," she added with a wink.

"I can't believe Aunt Georgia went home knowing she didn't have power and A/C."

"Believe it or not, she was anxious to get back and make sure her house was still standing and didn't care if she had to rough it for a few days. You know how she feels about that place."

And Mallory did. Her aunt loved to throw parties at her home and was always doing upgrades and renovations to it. It was watching her aunt that had originally gotten her into decorating. She remembered how they used to go shopping when she was little and it always fascinated her how her aunt always seemed to find the perfect items for her home. It was a showplace and Mallory was glad it was left unscathed from the hurricane.

"I'm fine with staying in town with them. I can handle a day without power," she said distractedly. The airport was about thirty miles from Magnolia Sound and with each mile they drove, her anxiety kicked up a notch. The thought of seeing the town ripped apart was going to be hard.

The thought of being there and knowing she was never going to see Pops again was almost more than she could bear.

"When will you be able to move back into...you know..."

Susannah looked over and gave her a sad smile. "Jake's going to have some engineers come out and look everything over. Being how it was just the addition that had the tree damage, it shouldn't affect the original structure. But with the deck coming down, he wants to make sure nothing else has been compromised." She paused. "Believe me, I wish we were going there instead of Beau and Georgia's. I'm ready to just have a little time to myself to come to grips with everything."

Mallory knew the feeling. She'd had a few days to let it all sink in, but what she wanted more than anything was some time here–at Pops' place–to have some time to herself to really accept the reality of the situation.

They drove in silence for several minutes.

"Jake said he went peacefully," Susannah said, breaking the quiet. "I'm glad it was like that for him and it wasn't the storm or an injury that..." Her voice cracked and Mallory turned to see tears streaming down her mother's face. "It doesn't seem real yet. Like I listened to Jake and we spoke to the coroner and there's still a part of me that keeps thinking it's all a mistake. I just can't believe he's gone!"

And now Mallory was crying too.

Not that it was hard to get her started again–this was probably the longest she'd gone between crying jags since she'd gotten the news. They both stayed quiet until they crossed the bridge that led to where the town of Magnolia Sound began.

"Mom?"

"Hmm?"

"Do you...do you think you can drop me off at the house? I mean, at Pops'."

Her mother turned and looked at her curiously. "You really shouldn't go in there until the engineers sign off on it..."

"No, I know. I just, I want to walk around the yard and just...I need some time. Please. I know it's a bit of an incon-venience since I don't have a car, but...I'm not ready to sit and talk with everyone. I know once we get to Aunt Georgia's, everyone's going to want to talk about the storm and the damage and I'd like to have some quiet time at the house. Alone." She glanced nervously at her mother. "Is that wrong? Am I being completely selfish?"

"Of course you're not being selfish. I completely understand! I just hate the thought of you seeing it all like that and not having anyone there to comfort you."

"I'll be okay." She smiled weakly. "This is just something that I have to do."

Susannah considered her for a moment. "Okay. Just... call or text me when you want me to come back."

"Thanks."

Tears continued to sting Mallory's eyes as she took in the devastation of the town as they drove down the main street. Sprinkles, which served the best ice cream she'd ever tasted, was boarded up and looked to be missing part of its roof. Beside it, the Bliss and Tell spa sat completely intact. The farther they drove, the sadder she felt. So many trees were gone. Houses sat in various stages of ruin while others went completely unharmed. It didn't seem fair, but then again, when had life been fair?

When her mother pulled into the grand driveway of Pops' home, Mallory gasped and started to cry all over again.

"Maybe you shouldn't do this right now," her mother said softly. "We can come back later...or maybe you can drive back on your own after we have some lunch..."

But she shook her head. "No. I need to do this now." And when the car came to a stop at the base of the steps leading up to the front porch, she turned to her mother and tried to smile. "Thank you. I'll call you in a bit."

When she stepped out onto the gravel drive, Mallory

waited until her mother had driven away before even taking one step. More than anything, she wanted to climb the steps and go into the house, but she knew she shouldn't. Although...looking around, it was obvious no one was here so...what harm would there be in just going inside and...

"No," she scolded herself. "Don't do it. Not yet." Instead, she slowly made her way around the exterior of the house–avoiding the side where the tree had crushed the structure–and into the back yard. The massive deck was a crumbled mess. It blocked the lower-level entry into the house and it broke her heart to see it looking like this. How many parties had they had up on that deck? How many times had she stood outside and leaned on the railing while staring out at the Sound?

Too many to even count.

They would rebuild it and it would be fine, but it would never be the same. Not ever.

With a weary sigh, she walked around the yard and didn't even try to fight the next wave of tears as she saw how the flooding had made a mess of Pops' garden. She remembered the last time they sat out here together in the big wooden swing and talked. He'd held her hand and listened to her ramble on about her job and seemed perfectly content to just listen to the sound of her voice. And she had been equally content to sit in that swing and listen to him talk about the old days in Magnolia Sound.

What a pair they made.

She'd give anything to hear one of his stories right now–to just hear the sound of his voice as she walked around or to know that once she turned around and went inside, he'd be there waiting to greet her with one of his big hugs.

"Oh, God," she sobbed, knowing it was never going to happen again. Why hadn't she come home this summer like she always did? How could she have let her own petty issues keep her from having one last visit with him? And now she had to live with that fact for the rest of her life.

Forcing herself to keep walking, she knew the yard was going to need almost as much work as the house. And even though it wasn't as important–making sure the house was structurally sound was the first priority–Mallory knew Pops would want his yard restored to its former glory. It was his pride and joy, this yard, and if she had to do it all herself, she'd make sure it looked just like it always did.

Well, she knew gardening wasn't really her thing, so she'd call Sam to come help. He was the gifted one in the family where this sort of thing was concerned. At least, that's what Pops had always said.

Her brother was going to be arriving in town some time tomorrow and she made a mental note to talk to him about staying here for a while or at least coming down on the weekends until the yard was completely restored.

Next she made her way down to the pier and breathed a sigh of relief when she saw that her mother was right–the boathouse was still intact. It had always been her special place here on the property and the fact that it went unscathed in such a fierce storm was a bit of a miracle.

Carefully, she stepped over the missing boards and slowly walked down toward the boathouse. Her heart was beating wildly the closer she got. There were so many memories attached to this place–different from the ones of just a moment ago. This was her spot–hers and Jake's–and a part of her would always think of it as such.

Touching the door, Mallory turned and decided not to go inside. Right now, she needed to be outside, breathing in the smells of the Sound and just...being. It seemed silly, but more than anything, this is what she needed to get herself together.

Every once in a while, she'd look over her shoulder toward the house and think she was going to see Pops out on the deck waving to her or that Gertie would come out and tell her lunch was ready.

As if on cue, her stomach growled and she cursed the fact that she hadn't eaten a proper breakfast this morning. Flying was not something she enjoyed doing and it seemed like the smart option not to eat until she got to Aunt Georgia's. Of course, that went out the window when she decided she needed to come here first.

Priorities...they were a little messed up at the moment and seemingly on their own emotional rollercoaster.

She was tired. Sleep had been an illusion ever since the storm hit and once she got the call about Pops...well...it hadn't gotten any better. The first thing Mallory had tried to do after getting the news was to get back here to be with her family, but with the storm moving up the East Coast, she'd had to wait. And driving wasn't an option because she didn't feel in control of her emotions to be on the road for that long.

Inhaling deeply, she held her breath for a moment before letting it out slowly. She repeated it several times before she felt herself begin to relax.

And she knew it would be an even longer time before she felt like her old self again.

Maybe it was the lack of sleep over the last several days or the fact that he hadn't been eating much, but Jake was fairly certain he was seeing a mirage. It was the only explanation he could come up with as to why he saw Mallory standing out on the pier beside the boathouse. He racked his brain to try to remember if anyone mentioned her coming home–coming here–but couldn't recall. Then again, there was so much going on that he was amazed he could remember his own name right now.

Standing exactly where he was and afraid to move or make a sound to spook her, Jake simply stood there and watched her. No doubt she was devastated and part of him longed to go to her and hold her, comfort her. In his mind it seemed like the right thing to do, but he had a feeling he wasn't the person she wanted to accept comfort of any kind from.

And whose fault is that?

Totally his and he had long since accepted this fact, but when faced with a situation like this one, he couldn't help but wish things were different.

She looked so sad and even from this distance, he could see she was crying. With her arms wrapped around her middle, she was the portrait of the grieving great-grand-daughter. Jake took a minute to look around the property. No one was here. The construction crews weren't due to come back until next week because they all had personal damage to deal with. From where he stood, he didn't see a car in the driveway so...how did she get here?

"Hell, maybe I am seeing things," he murmured, scratching his head in confusion. And then he did the only thing he could do–he walked down to the pier to either confirm or deny that Mallory was really there.

The moment his foot hit the pier, she turned toward him and for a moment, Jake was afraid to move any closer. She looked like a deer caught in the headlights, but he refused to let that stop him. Now that he knew he wasn't imagining things, he needed to go make sure she was all right.

Or as all right as she could be, considering the current circumstances.

Jake slowly made his way down the pier and waited for Mallory to say something or to even look away, but she didn't. When he was beside her, he simply said, "Hey."

"Hey," she replied softly.

She'd definitely been crying and now he felt like a jerk for coming here and interrupting her. A ton of questions came to his mind, but they all seemed trite. "Sorry to disturb you," he finally said. "I...I was just surprised to see you down here. I didn't realize you were coming in so soon. Wasn't sure the roads were clear leading in and out of town yet."

Nodding, she turned and looked out at the water. "I just got in. Mom picked me up at the airport and I asked her to drop me off here. I wanted...no, I needed to come here and sort of see things for myself."

He nodded too because he understood. "It's a lot to take in."

"It still doesn't seem real. Like, I keep waiting to wake up and have someone tell me it's all been a terrible dream." She looked at him with a sad smile. "Any chance of that happening?"

His heart squeezed hard. "Afraid not, Mal." And then as if of one mind, they moved toward each other and he held her as she cried. She burrowed in close and Jake's arms banded around her. It was familiar and comforting and yet...different. They weren't the same people who had once stood embracing on this same pier years ago, but...

Now wasn't the time to be focusing on that.

Even if it was a great distraction from the hell they were currently living with.

When Mallory pulled back a few minutes later, she immediately began wiping the tears away before she took several steps to put some distance between them. "Um...sorry. I can't seem to stop doing that."

"Totally understandable. I've done more than my share in the last several days too." Her look of surprise told him maybe he shouldn't have admitted that, but...he couldn't take it back. "I was here with him, Mal. It was...it was the hardest moment of my life." Tears started to well in her eyes again and he cursed himself for bring this up so soon. "I mean..."

But she held up a hand to stop him. "I can't. I can't hear about it. Not yet. Please."

With a curt nod, he turned and looked out at the water, relieved that the Sound was going down more and more each day. It would be a long while before everything was back to normal, but at least this was progress he could immediately see.

"So... where are you staying?"

"With Uncle Beau and Aunt Georgia. At least for now." She paused. "I was hoping we'd get the okay to stay here in the house, but I'm sure it's going to take a while before your engineers give us permission."

He made a mental note to call in some favors and see if he could make that happen for her.

"We have the option to stay at the townhouse where everyone stayed during the storm, but...I don't know, I feel like I need to be here in town."

"I get it. Has anyone talked about...you know...the funeral?" As soon as the words were out, he wished he could take them back. The look of devastation on Mallory's face gutted him. How could he keep messing up and saying all the wrong things? He was about to apologize or at least try to change the subject when she spoke.

"We're all going to talk about it tonight. At least, that's the plan. Everyone's supposed to get together for dinner, but with no power and things being such a mess, I'm not sure if it's still going to happen."

They stood like that for what felt like forever before he realized just how hot it was outside. There was no direct sun–the skies were still gray and overcast–but he knew he was getting uncomfortable. "Would you like something to drink?" he asked. "I have a generator over at my place and while I don't have a whole lot to choose from, at least it will be cold."

She considered him for a long moment before agreeing. "Thank you. That would be nice."

Together they walked back up the pier and at one point he reached for her hand to help her over some of the missing boards, but once they were back on the massive lawn, Mallory gently pulled her hand away. It was odd how much he wanted to grab it back.

"How did your place fare during the storm? Did you get much damage?" she asked.

"Other than losing some roofing shingles and some of the siding coming loose, the house itself made out okay. The property, just like Zeke's, took the harder hit. There are so many trees and some of them just weren't big enough to sustain the winds and then once we had all the flooding, so many of them just toppled over because of the saturated ground." He shrugged and stepped over several fallen branches, then turned to help Mallory. "Shallow roots are really to blame in cases like this."

It was small talk at its best, but Jake figured he'd better

stick to safer topics after his numerous fails down on the pier.

They climbed up the back steps to the house and Jake opened the door for her and followed her inside. She froze after only a few steps and he walked right into her. "Oof!"

Mallory gasped and then turned, blushing adorably. "Sorry. I just...everything looks so different since I was here last."

Jake stepped around her as he walked over to the refrigerator and pulled out a couple of bottles of water, handing one to her. "When I bought the place from my folks two years ago, everything was seriously outdated. So this became my weekend project. I do a little something here and there." He shrugged, opening his water. "Kind of like a labor of love. And besides, the place really needed it."

She nodded but didn't comment, taking a long drink of her water instead.

He motioned for her to sit down and noticed she was still curiously looking around. "You can walk around and check it all out if you'd like. Besides the kitchen and living room, I turned one of the bedrooms into an office and just started on the main bathroom."

Without looking at him, Mallory walked around the living room. She touched the built-in bookcases he'd made and ran a hand over the new mantle over the fireplace. While the structure of the house was good, he knew the décor left a lot to be desired. This was still the furniture his parents had from when he was growing up and someday he'd replace it, but for now it was fine and functional. He figured she was looking around and redecorating the room in her mind and it made him smile.

"You think I should go with a sectional in here or a sofa and loveseat?" he asked, stepping into the space.

"A sectional," she said without hesitation. "Something light and, knowing you, you're going to want an even bigger television over the fireplace, right?"

Laughing, he nodded. "It was going to be a Christmas present to myself this year."

"I went to visit Sam a couple of months ago and his TV seemed to fill up an entire wall!" she said, laughing with him. "I questioned him on it but then he proceeded to educate me on the importance of the big screen. Needless to say, I don't love it from a decorating standpoint, but I understand it from an entertainment one."

"The funny thing is I don't watch a lot of TV, but when I do, I guess it will be nice. Although, for years I got by with this one and ones much smaller so...I'll live if I never upgrade."

Mallory moved around the room, looking at the framed family pictures he had on the bookshelves. "I don't know about that. I think you should fill your home with things you want–things that make you happy." She paused and moved over to the other built-in and examined those pictures. "Just last week I was looking around my place and thinking how I wish I could go on decorating it over and over. Or maybe just get a second place to decorate because I love to do it."

"I remember," he said softly and Mallory turned to look at him, her eyes a little wide. Shrugging, Jake went on, "I remember how much fun you had working on Zeke's office and then the boathouse. You spent a lot of time that summer shopping for the perfect pieces of furniture and the perfect paintings and accessories." He chuckled. "At the time I thought you were crazy, but I couldn't argue with the finished product. It all looked great."

Neither moved for a minute and once again, Jake had to wonder if he should have just kept his mouth shut. Then again, they couldn't just pretend their past didn't happen. It did. They had a history together and there were memories he was unwilling to never mention again.

No matter how uncomfortable it may make her.

Finally, Mallory said, "Thank you." She walked back through the kitchen and then down the hall to his office. She stood in the doorway and Jake followed. "Did you make the desk yourself?" Her lips twitched with amusement.

"Um...yeah." Truth was, it was a plastic folding table with a piece of plywood over it. He didn't really need anything more, but he supposed a real desk might not be a bad investment. "I found it down in the garage and it does what I need it to do."

She shook her head. "I do like what you did with the walls. The color is great and it's impressive how you did built-ins in here without making them look the same as the ones in the living room. I didn't realize carpentry was your thing."

He shrugged again. "Don't get me wrong, designing and building on a bigger scale is always going to be what I want to do, but I love projects like this and how I can personalize it exactly the way I want."

For a minute she went completely still and then seemed to sway on her feet. When she looked ready to fall, Jake stepped in and put his arms around her. "Mal? You okay?" he asked frantically.

Placing a hand on her forehead, she nodded. "I skipped breakfast this morning and I think it's really catching up with me." She didn't move away from him right away, but did fumble for her purse. "I should probably call my mother and ask her to come back and get me. It's well after lunchtime, but I'm sure Aunt Georgia has something I can throw together."

"Have lunch with me," he blurted out before thinking it through. Her shocked expression didn't deter him. "I haven't eaten yet and was going to make a sandwich or something. You're more than welcome to join me."

He had forgotten just how expressive her face could be. Then again, he also knew how polite Mallory was and knew that even if she didn't want to have lunch with him, she wouldn't turn him down.

"Thanks, but...I think I'll just call Mom and go grab something with her and the family."

Okay...maybe he didn't know her as well as he once thought.

"Um...what?"

She moved to put some distance between them again and sighed. "I appreciate the invitation, but..."

"Look, can't we put...you know...the past aside? For the next week or so that you're undoubtedly going to be here, we're going to be seeing each other." He waited to see if she'd interrupt or argue, but she didn't. "There was a time when we were friends, Mal, and I'd really like it if we could be again. Now more than ever, I think it's important. I know Zeke would have wanted that."

And yeah, he knew he was playing dirty, but desperate times and all.

It took less than a second for her to look away and pull her phone out of her purse. Reaching out, he put a hand on her arm. "C'mon, Mallory. Please."

And then she did look at him and he hated what he saw—pain, sadness, and distrust.

He immediately stepped back and motioned for her to make her call and he went back to the kitchen to give her privacy.

Sitting down at the kitchen table, he sighed. What the

hell was he supposed to do? They were going to have to get past this. They had a history long before they were involved and as long as he lived here and her family continued to live next door then...

What if it didn't happen? What if now that Zeke was gone, Susannah and Georgia and whoever else was involved decided to sell the house? Then he'd never see Mallory again.

Then again, judging by how quickly she was looking to get away from him, he doubted she'd be too disappointed if that happened.

"Thanks, Mom. I'll see you in a few minutes," he heard her say just as she walked back into the kitchen. When she spotted him, she came to a halt and placed her phone back in her purse. "Um...I need to go back over to Pops' place. I told my mother I'd meet her out front."

He came to his feet and felt more than a little annoyed with the way she was running away. But then again, should he really be surprised? "You could have just told her to come here. There's a lot less debris on my property and it would be easier for her to get in and out."

"We did fine earlier. Really, it's okay." She walked over to the back door before looking at him again. "Thanks for the water and...I guess I'll see you around."

"Mallory, wait," he said, going to her. This time he did reach for her and didn't care if she looked shocked or not. "This is ridiculous!" Grasping her shoulders, he held her just close enough that he could feel the warmth of her body, but far enough that there was still some space between them. "I'm not going to spend the rest of my life worrying about you avoiding me or dealing with you refusing to talk to me! We're adults, dammit!"

When she went to pull out of his grasp, he held on even

tighter–his fingers digging into her skin. "Thanks for the reminder," she all but spat at him. "I almost forgot how immature you think I am."

Oh for the love of it...

This time when she went to pull away, he dragged her in close until they were chest to chest. "Stop it," he growled. "That was a long time ago and we need to let it go!"

She glared at him.

"I've already let it go. You're the one who brought it up," she snapped, still wiggling and trying to move away.

He should have just let her go–should have just said goodbye and let her go on her way–but he couldn't. Now that she was this close, Jake lost all sense of what was right and wrong, along with all sense of reason.

"More than anything, right now we should be doing our best to get along," he said, forcing himself to ignore how good she felt against him–how good she smelled, how soft her skin was under his hands.

"Oh, please," she said, rolling her eyes. "Don't even go there. Our getting along has nothing to do with anything anymore." Once more she tried to pull away from him and Jake could see how frustrated she was when he wouldn't let go. "Dammit, Jake! Stop it!"

The only thing her movements managed to do was to put her firmly against him. Her breasts were crushed against his chest and they were both breathing heavily at the exertion. He stared long and hard at her and the only thing going through his mind was that if they were going to do this–if they were going to move on the way he said they needed to, then he needed to do this one last thing to get her out of his system.

He hauled her in impossibly closer and kissed her.

4

Mallory forgot to be outraged as she dropped her purse and raked her hands up into Jake's hair.

It was better than she remembered–all of it–the silkiness of his hair, the way his hands ran up and down her back, and most of all, his kiss. She completely melted against him and reveled in the feeling of having Jake wrapped around her. The feel of his lips on hers, the way his tongue teased and tangled with hers…it was enough to make Mallory completely forget where she was.

He backed her up until they were out of the doorway, but they didn't go any further. Once her back hit the wall, it was all she could do to keep from wrapping her legs around his hips and begging for more. It had always been this way– one kiss was enough to trigger a thousand sensations and it was amazing how her body still responded to his after all this time.

Hands roamed, tongues dueled, and still it wasn't enough. She needed to breathe–needed to simply break the kiss and gasp for air–but she couldn't make herself do it.

The thought of losing their connection–even for a minute–was too great of a risk to take.

Unfortunately, Jake was willing to take that risk and when he broke the kiss and panted breathlessly against her throat, saying her name, sanity started to return.

What am I doing?

His mouth moved along her jaw. He gently bit her throat as he seemed desperate to keep his lips on her. There was a little voice inside of her telling her to stop this madness–to move away and get control of the situation. But then there was another little voice totally telling her to arch her back and press into him and let Jake keep doing what he was doing.

That was the voice she ultimately listened to.

When Jake bent and kissed his way down her throat to the vee of her blouse, Mallory silently prayed he'd simply rip the buttons apart so he could kiss her breasts–but he didn't. Instead he kissed her over the fabric, but she felt his teeth scrape against her nipple and her knees practically buckled.

Opening one eye, she saw the sofa was less than ten feet away. They could be there in a matter of seconds, right? Maybe if she nudged him, she could get him to move so they could...

Her thoughts were interrupted by the ringing of her phone. It took a minute for her to gather her wits and make her body move away from his. She gently pushed him back as she bent down and picked up her purse, and clumsily fished her cellphone out.

Her mother.

Muttering a curse, she quickly answered. "Hey, Mom. Sorry. I'll be out in a minute, okay?"

"Are you okay, Mallory?" her mother asked, concerned. "You sound out of breath."

She looked guiltily at Jake, who was studying her with such heated intensity that she almost hung up on her mother so she could go back to kissing him. Her body moved of its own accord toward him when she heard, "Mallory? Are you there?"

Another curse. "Yeah, sorry. There's a lot of debris back here and I'm trying to be careful. I'll talk to you in a minute, okay?"

"Okay. Take your time. I'm enjoying the air conditioning in the car," Susannah said with amusement.

Hanging up, she slid the phone back into her purse and took a step back toward the door. "Um...I need to go."

Jake took a step toward her and Mallory wished he wouldn't. The closer he got, the more she wanted to just reach out, grab his shirt and pull him to her.

"You should have let me drive you home," he said, his voice low and gruff.

She shook her head. "No. It's better this way. I...we... this shouldn't have happened." Looking over her shoulder and out the door, she knew she needed to go. "She's waiting so..."

It happened so fast that she never saw it coming. Jake grabbed her and kissed her one last time. It was so sudden and intense that it left her feeling dizzy. He steadied her before stepping away. "This isn't over, Mal. I thought it was...thought we could just do that and prove there was nothing there, but..."

She held up a hand to stop him. Yeah, she knew exactly what he was going to say and already knew she couldn't argue it. It was true. There was still something there between them, but it was just physical.

Just as it had been all those years ago.

The physical part of their relationship had never been the problem

It was the emotional part that never seemed to work.

And it clearly wasn't working right now either.

"I can't deal with this right now, Jake," she said. "There's so much going on – so many things I have to focus on and...I...I just need to go." And before he could do or say anything else, Mallory was out the door and making her way quickly and carefully across the property to meet her mother.

A few minutes later, she breathlessly climbed into the waiting car. "Sorry."

Susannah studied her daughter for a long moment. "Are you okay?"

Mallory nodded and wished they'd start driving. "I'm starving, actually, and feeling a bit light-headed. Please tell me Aunt Georgia has something I can put together for lunch."

"There's all the makings for sandwiches and plenty of snacks." She glanced over at Mallory again. "Are you sure that's all this is? Hunger?"

Now that was a loaded question. But rather than say anything, she nodded.

"You saw Jake, didn't you?" It wasn't a question.

Why deny it? Watching the scenery go by as they finally pulled out of the driveway, she replied, "Yeah. I was down on the pier and he came down to make sure I was okay."

"Well that was nice of him."

Mallory wasn't so sure she could agree.

"How was he doing?" her mother asked. "I saw him yesterday and he was really...well, I think he's taking the loss just as hard as the rest of us. He and Pops were always close."

"He seemed fine."

"Hmm..."

That had her turning her head. "What? What did that mean?"

"What did what mean?"

"Your little hum."

Her mother shrugged. "It was nothing."

"Mom..." she whined.

They drove in silence for a few minutes until Mallory thought she'd go mad. It wasn't until they were parked in Georgia and Beau's driveway that her mother responded. "There was a time when Jake Summerford was your entire world," she began. "You kept that secret hidden from me fairly well before the two of you became a couple and well into the relationship." She paused. "Sometimes relationships—romantic ones—don't work out the way we want them to. And in the case of you and Jake, I think it was a case of bad timing. But now more than anything it's important to remember you're friends who are both grieving over the same thing—the person who meant so much to the both of you. Maybe it's time to stop looking at all that went wrong with the two of you and focus on helping each other now when you both need it."

It was the last thing she ever expected to hear from her mother, who had always been very supportive of her feelings. "I don't think Jake and I were ever really friends, Mom. I think I just happened to be his neighbor's great-granddaughter who he saw once a year." It hurt to say it, but she'd come to grips with it a long time ago.

Or at least...she thought she had.

Beside her, her mother shrugged. "I can't answer that

for you, Mallory, but I think the coming weeks are going to be hard on everyone and maybe you should try to put any hard feelings aside where Jake is concerned. He... well...I can't even imagine how he must have felt when he found Pops." She shuddered. "And then he had to take on the task of calling us and breaking the news...I'm telling you, I wouldn't wish that sort of thing on anyone. And through it all he's been incredibly gracious and helpful and..."

"I get it, Mom. I do. It's the worst situation I can ever imagine for anyone. My heart breaks for him having gone through what he did and I promise I'll be more considerate of his feelings."

"That wasn't quite what I was saying..."

"No, no...I get it. I have been kind of bratty where he's concerned these last several years and if I had just been more mature, I would have come to visit Pops back in June like I always did. Now I missed out and I'll never get to..." She cursed as the tears started to fall. "I really wish I could stop crying all the damn time!"

Susannah reached over and hugged her. "In time you will. We all will. Right now it's all too new and you're allowed to grieve, sweetheart. Don't feel bad about that."

They stayed like that until there was a loud knock on the car window. Breaking apart, Mallory spotted her cousin Mason and smiled. As much as he used to annoy her, right now he was the perfect distraction.

"Come on," Susannah said. "Let's go inside and get you something to eat."

Climbing out of the car, Mallory thanked her cousin who was holding the door for her. "Hey, you," she said, hugging him. "How are you?"

Hugging her back before releasing her, Mason gave her

a small smile. "You know, getting by. This week has been…" He stopped and let out a long breath.

"I know." She studied him and realized he'd changed so much in the last couple of years. He still towered over her, but his looks finally changed from that of a boy to a man– which really shouldn't surprise her. He was only a year younger than Mallory, but gone was her younger cousin and in his place was a very respectful – and beefed up - looking man. Not that he had much choice than to look respectful. Mallory knew her aunt and uncle expected a lot from their only son and he clearly took it to heart.

"I brought your luggage in earlier when Aunt Susannah first got back. You're in Parker's room since she's not home yet," he said, walking beside her up to the house. Mallory noted her mother had already gone inside and she held Mason back before going in.

"Can I ask you something?"

His brows furrowed slightly. "Sure."

She hesitated for a minute. "Do you think I should have gone to stay at a hotel or maybe at your townhouse where everyone was during the storm? I don't want to be a burden or in the way here."

Mason laughed and his sandy brown hair blew slightly in the wind. "Mal, are you crazy? Why would you even ask such a thing? You know my mother gets off on playing the hostess—even when the circumstances are a little rough like they are now. You'd think she was throwing a cotillion rather than having the family over to plan a damn funeral."

That did sound exactly like her aunt, but she still felt a little out of place being here. Maybe it was because when-ever she had come to visit during all those summers, she had always stayed at Pops' house. The idea of not being there while being so close by left her feeling slightly unsettled.

"There's plenty of room and we have a guarantee that the power will be back on by tomorrow–if not later today. And I think my sisters are both going to be back in the next couple of days but even when they do, there's still going to be plenty of room for you." He hugged her again briefly. "We're all happy that you're here so stop worrying."

"I know Sam's coming in tomorrow too..."

"Oh, right," Mason said, his expression changing slightly. "There's room for him too. I think he'll end up on the sleeper sofa down in the den, but it's still kind of private. Plus, it will be good to have someone else here to help me with the cleanup. I swear, my folks haven't given me a break since we got back yesterday."

Laughing, Mallory playfully punched him in the arm. "That's what you get for being the big, strong one in the family!"

He rolled his eyes. "Right. More like that's what I get for not being smart like my sisters and getting the hell out of town before the storm hit." He laughed, but she had a feeling he wasn't really joking.

"Are you planning on settling here in Magnolia now that you're done with college or are you going to move?"

He shrugged. "I do love it here and I know I need to find a place of my own, but..." He shrugged and gave her a lopsided grin. "Can't beat the free rent, free meals, and laundry service."

Mallory couldn't help but laugh. "Oh my gosh...you sound just like Sam. Always looking for the easy way out."

Mason's grin grew. "Yeah, but he moved far away from home once he was through with college so clearly he doesn't think like that anymore."

"You'd be surprised," she murmured.

"Come on, let's get inside before everyone starts wondering what we're plotting and planning out here."

She laughed but thought the comment was odd. Looking over her shoulder at him as they walked up to the door, she asked, "What could anyone think we'd be plotting?"

Mason shrugged and gave her a small nudge into the house, but Mallory could have sworn she heard him murmur, "Escaping."

"I know I'm asking a lot, Jerry, but I need you to make this happen," Jake said firmly, ready to rip his own hair out of his head.

"Do you have any idea how many places are in worse condition and require immediate attention?" Jerry replied with just enough snap to his voice to let Jake know he was equally frustrated. "I've had more phone calls from friends and relatives asking for favors so they can get back into their homes. If I helped each and every one of them..."

And then he knew he had to play just a little dirty if he was going to get what he wanted. "Zeke Coleman gave you a start in this business twenty years ago, Jerry. Remember that? And I happen to know that during those twenty years, you've done your fair share of messing around and nearly losing your job. Yet Zeke always gave you a second, third, and even fourth chance. Hell, he paid for rehab for you or have you forgotten that?"

There was silence for a minute and then Jerry cursed. "Yeah. He did."

"The house is a historical landmark in this town and even though Zeke will never walk through those doors again, his family will. It would mean a lot to them–and me–if you would go over there today and check it out to make sure it's safe for them to go in to."

"There's a tree down on the front corner, Jake! You said it yourself!"

"It's the addition and it has no bearing on the main structure. Clear the main structure–or at least make sure it's safe for Susannah and her family to get in there."

"And if it's not? I'm not going to lie, Jake."

That would be a first, he thought, but kept it to himself. "I'm not asking you to lie. I'm asking you to go and check it out so *if* it is safe, I can call Susannah and let her know she can move back in. And if it's not, I'll know what I'm looking at for getting a crew in there ASAP."

"Didn't you used to date Susannah's daughter?"

"Not the point, Jerry," he snapped. "This is about doing Zeke a solid and looking after his family the same way he looked after yours. Are we clear?"

"Yeah. I'm actually not far from there now. I can meet you in about twenty minutes."

"Good. Thanks." When he hung up, Jake flung his phone on the sofa beside him with disgust. He hated calling in favors and worse, hated anyone questioning his motives. The fact was that he *was* doing this for Zeke. The sooner the house was back in shape, the better he'd feel.

I'm doing this so Zeke can rest in peace and know his family was being taken care of.

Jake placed a hand over his heart and rubbed his chest. The pain was so raw, so fresh, and he didn't know if he'd ever get past it. The only thing saving his sanity right now was the fact that there was so much to do–so much of Magnolia Sound that was going to need to be rebuilt–that he knew he wouldn't have time to mourn.

Hell, it was going to be a matter of survival–working himself into exhaustion so he could simply come home at the end of the day and crash.

Good luck with that, he thought. Zeke touched every single thing in this town. He might not have continued to own everything here, but he owned enough that he left one hell of a legacy. It would be impossible to drive through town and not think of his old friend.

In the last several years, Zeke had handed off so much of his daily operations to competent managers–Jake being one of them–but he'd be lying if he wasn't curious about how things were going to move forward without the input of the man who started it all. He had no doubt that arrangements had been made and in the coming weeks everyone would know where they stood, but Jake wondered if the construction company was going to stay as-is with a new CEO in Zeke's place or if it was going to be sold, along with so many other businesses here in town.

His hand moved from his chest to his temple as a headache began to take root. There was so much to think about and it didn't matter how much there was to do because right there in the back of his mind was what happened earlier with Mallory.

"You just had to go and kiss her, didn't you," he chided himself. It was a reckless move and he knew he should regret doing it, but he couldn't. They had been dancing around each other for too damn long and he was sick of it. Yeah, things ended badly and yeah, he was mostly to blame for that, but the bottom line was that they were both guilty parties in it. It wasn't all his fault and it wasn't all hers, so why couldn't they sit down and talk about it? Or just talk in general! Why did that one summer have to mean they could never be friends again?

Sighing, he rested his head back against the sofa cushions and closed his eyes. Hell, he could still taste her on his lips and feel her pressed against him. It was freaking maddening. Six damn years! When was it going to end?

Probably when you stop obsessing about her and kissing her, you idiot.

Yeah, there was that.

In the four years he was away at school, Jake certainly hadn't lived like a monk, but he hadn't gotten serious with anyone either. And when he finally came home, life had gotten complicated with his parents wanting to retire, him buying the house, and settling back into life here in Magnolia. Getting updates on Mallory from Zeke hadn't been hard, but he never expected her to skip any of her annual visits the way she did this year. And he'd be lying if he said he didn't feel a twinge of guilt knowing he was more than likely the reason she didn't come home–because without a doubt she was going to beat herself up for not coming and seeing her great-grandfather before he died.

Something they'd have to deal with eventually...

His phone ringing brought him out of his reverie and he couldn't help but smile when he saw his father's number on the screen. "Hey, Dad," he said, thankful for a bit of a distraction.

"Hey, I was just calling to check on you and see how you're doing. Has the cleanup started around town yet?" Jonah Summerford asked.

"Not much yet, but the flood waters have finally receded and roads are getting cleared of debris so I'm sure in the next day or two we'll hit it full force."

"I hate the thought of all that destruction. In all the years we lived there..." He paused. "Well, you know."

"It could have been a lot worse, Dad. For all that we lost

around here, I still consider us lucky. Other spots up and down the coast have much more to deal with. And luckily, it can all be rebuilt."

"The structures can, sure. But the people..."

Jake didn't have to ask what his father meant. "Yeah, that one's never going to go away," he said quietly. "I don't think there are many spots in this town that don't have a connection to Zeke and it's going to be a long time before we'll get over his loss."

"I'm not sure if any of us will ever get over it," his father said solemnly. "Only once in a lifetime do you meet someone like Ezekiel Coleman and I know his legacy will go on long after most of us are gone."

"Amen to that."

"How's his family doing? Have you talked to Susannah? I know she's been living with him and I'm sure this has to be particularly hard on her."

Jake relayed all the family news – including the fact that Mallory was back and they were supposed to start making funeral plans.

"And how do you feel about that?"

"Dad, I knew there was going to be a funeral."

"Not that. Mallory. How did that go?"

There was no way he was going to share what had happened earlier. "It's fine," he lied. "It's not like I didn't expect her to be here and...we have seen each other a time or two over the years, so..."

"Uh-huh."

"What? What's with the uh-huh?"

"I'm just wondering how long it's going to take before you realize you made a huge mistake where Mallory is concerned."

So not the conversation he wanted to have right now.

"Dad..."

"Yeah, yeah, yeah...I know. That's not why I called and I know you have a million other things on your mind. I really just wanted to call and make sure you're doing okay. Your mother and I worry. That's all."

Jake felt himself sag with relief. "Thanks, Dad. I'm doing okay. Sometimes it all just hits me and then..."

"I know."

They were silent for a moment before Jonah asked, "Do you want us to come home for the funeral?"

Jake hadn't really even considered that. His folks were always close with the Coleman's and it made sense that they'd want to be here to pay their respects, but...

"That's completely up to you, Dad. I don't have any of the details and things here in town are crazy, but you know you're always welcome here. My house is your house," he said with a small chuckle. "Literally and figuratively."

Jonah laughed too. "Well, we've been talking about it and didn't want to add to the chaos there. We're going to send flowers and reach out to the family, but if you want us there, we'll be on the next flight."

And there wasn't a doubt in Jake's mind that they would. However...

"I think sending flowers would be real nice, Dad. You know Zeke wouldn't want you to go out of your way or inconvenience yourself."

Jonah laughed again. "I know. That's what I keep telling myself, but I can't help but feel a little guilty. Plus, if we came home, we'd get to see you."

"There's so much to be done around here that I'm not sure we'd even get to spend any time together. My phone hasn't stopped ringing and my to-do list is a mile long. All the work that lies ahead will keep me focused and I'm actually looking forward to getting started." Which reminded him... "I'm meeting an engineer over at Zeke's place. I'm hoping to get clearance for Susannah to move back in. He's going to be there any minute, so..."

"Don't let me keep you," Jonah said. "Go and do what you need to do. We're thinking of you and if there's anything you need, just ask."

"I appreciate that and I'll talk to you soon."

Once Jake hung up, he rested his head back, closed his eyes, and wished he could just sleep for a day or two. Unfortunately, that wasn't possible. Forcing himself to get up, he went into the kitchen and made himself a quick sandwich before he had to go over and meet up with Jerry. With any luck, they would find the old house stable enough for Susannah to move back in and then make a plan for doing the repairs on the addition and the deck. It wouldn't be quick and it wouldn't be soon, but right now it was going to be his main priority.

Throwing the sandwich together, he took a bite and frowned. He'd kill for a real meal. For days this is all he'd been eating and while he was thankful for it, he was just ready to eat something that you couldn't place between two slices of bread. A nice steak or perhaps some fish would be his goal for tomorrow—something he could grill and eat hot. His mind wandered to all the things he was going to cook once all the power was back on and things began to return to normal.

Unfortunately, none of those thoughts were helping him choke down his meal any easier, so rather than obsess about food, he grabbed his tablet and began making notes on what he was going to ask Jerry about as they walked around Zeke's place. With any luck, he could call Susannah and have her back in the house by dinnertime or at the latest, tomorrow morning.

He remembered Mallory mentioning how they were having a family meeting tonight to discuss Zeke's funeral, so maybe he'd text Susannah rather than calling to make sure he didn't interrupt anything important.

Then he thought about calling Mallory instead. It was a legitimate excuse for a call–letting her know she could get back into Zeke's house–but...to what end? What was he hoping to get out of calling her?

Okay, the answer was fairly obvious–more of what happened today. But beyond that, he had to think about what was practical. There was so much going on right now and once again, the timing wasn't good for them. She was here for a short period of time right now and then she would go back to her home and job up in New York and he would still be here with more work than he knew what to do with. So again, why was he looking to pursue anything?

Good question.

Finishing his sandwich, he quickly cleaned up the kitchen, grabbed his phone and tablet, and headed for the door. And only one answer came to mind...

Because I need to get her out of my system...

Mallory looked down at the phone in her hands and blinked.

Jake: Main house passed inspection. You can move back in tonight.

She was sitting at her aunt's massive dining room table surrounded by most of her family and she hated to interrupt the conversation to tell them about Jake's message.

Her uncle was sitting at the head of the table and was currently talking about the conversation he had earlier with the funeral home. Mallory couldn't make herself focus on it. It was too much. She hated thinking of Pops being somewhere like that–even though she knew it was exactly the way things needed to be. He was cold and alone and the thought of it broke her heart.

Beside her, her mother glanced over. "Everything okay?" Mallory held up the phone and showed her Jake's text. With a small smile, she said, "It's wonderful news."

"What is?" Aunt Georgia asked, clearly not listening to her husband either.

"Oh, um...Jake Summerford just sent word that he had inspectors out at the house and the main structure passed inspection. Mallory and I can move back over tonight if we want."

Georgia's face pinched just ever-so-slightly before she put a smile back in place. "Are you sure that's a good idea? There is still so much damage all around with the deck being gone and the front wing being crushed."

"The front wing is only partially crushed," Susannah corrected mildly, "and we would just keep that part of the house closed off for now. I know I'd feel better just going over and doing a walk-through myself. Not that I don't trust Jake or the engineers, but it'd help give me my own peace of mind."

"Well...no one's throwing you out of here, Susannah," Georgia said pleasantly. She was the epitome of the typical Southern belle who was always gracious, with a smile on her face even when she was mad as hell.

And Mallory had a feeling her aunt was mad right now because for years it had been well known that she had wanted Pops' house for herself. When Susannah had moved down to help care for Pops, all of Georgia's plans were put on hold.

Hopefully indefinitely.

"And I appreciate your hospitality," her mother said with a smile of her own. "And if it's okay with you, I will stay here tonight. Tomorrow, though, I'm hoping the power will be restored and we can start letting life return to normal."

At that point, Uncle Beau went back to talking about the plans he had discussed with the funeral director – visitations, flowers, a suit for Pops - and Mallory couldn't take it anymore. When she pushed her chair back and went to stand, everyone stopped talking and looked over at her.

"Sorry, but...I just need to go get some air," she said apologetically. Then she looked at her mother. "Can I borrow your car?"

"Why don't you go over and walk through the house?" her mother suggested. "I think we both know that's where you're going to go."

Smiling sadly, Mallory nodded. "Thanks." Then she looked up at everyone. "I'll see you all later."

It took less than five minutes for her to get her things and be in the car, pulling out of the driveway. The sun was setting and she realized a little too late that she wasn't going to have much daylight to help her see things in the house. Surely she'd be able to find a flashlight or something if she needed it, right?

When she pulled up in front of Pops' house, she didn't pause or hesitate. She was practically frantic to get inside.

Once she was through the front door, she realized she was breathless and shaking.

There was no one to call out to and no one to respond.

Walking slowly, she peeked into Pops' office and couldn't bring herself to stop. The house was eerily quiet and when she looked at the closed door to the downstairs wing, she was almost relieved. She wasn't sure she'd be able to handle seeing his room right now.

By the time she walked around the downstairs, she realized it was almost pointless to be here. Her thoughts were scattered in what felt like a million different directions and with the fading sunlight, there wasn't anything she could even do. Going to the kitchen pantry, she found a flashlight and took it with her before walking out the front door. She closed and locked it behind her and decided that maybe a little time down at the boathouse would be better for her.

Careful of the multiple fallen branches, Mallory walked around the side of the house and down to the pier. Sunsets were always beautiful out here and even with the overcast sky, she knew she would sit up on the party deck and enjoy it.

Down the pier and up the ladder to the deck she climbed and tossed her purse down on the floor. None of the furniture was up here so it wasn't like she had somewhere to sit, but it didn't matter. Standing at the rail looking out at the water was exactly what she wanted.

Closing her eyes, she inhaled deeply and let the breath out slowly, feeling all the tension leave her body. If she could, she'd camp out right here tonight and skip going back to her aunt and uncle's house. It wasn't anything personal; this was just the kind of mental health therapy she needed at the moment.

Between this reprieve from her hectic work life and her

grief over Pops, Mallory knew she'd take this kind of alone time over anything else. This had always been her happy place—the only place she ever felt like she could come and truly relax. At least, for a long time that had been the case. After her breakup with Jake, the boathouse held too many memories—ones she didn't want to think about. But after their kiss earlier, it was really no surprise she ended up here.

It was also no surprise when she heard footsteps on the pier.

Jake.

She didn't move. Hell, she had to make sure she was even breathing by the time he was up on the deck beside her.

"What are you doing up here?" he asked quietly, looking out at the Sound just as she was.

"I had to get out of there. They were talking about the funeral and…I just couldn't. It was too much."

Beside her, he let out a long breath. "In my head, I knew this day would come. Knew we'd be facing a day when Zeke wasn't here anymore. The reality of it is much harder than I thought it would be."

Unable to speak, Mallory simply nodded.

They stood like that for a long time. The sky was almost dark and she couldn't see much of anything anymore, but she could feel Jake beside her. More than anything, she wanted to lean into him and feel him wrap his arms around her and tell her everything was going to be okay. Logically, she knew it would—knew she would always mourn the loss of Pops—but right now she wanted comfort and to just…feel something other than grief.

Turning her head, she looked at him and gasped softly when she saw he was already looking at her. "Jake," she whispered, but had no idea what else to say.

Reaching out, he cupped her cheek, caressed it. She leaned into his hand, loving how rough his skin felt against hers. She'd always loved that about him, the fact that he worked with his hands and they were so large and rough. It's funny how up until this moment she hadn't realized how much she missed that.

"You staying at the house tonight?" he asked, his voice no more than a whisper too.

She shook her head. "I think we're coming back tomorrow. I'm supposed to stay with everyone over at my aunt's place tonight."

He stepped in closer and Mallory's eyes fluttered shut at how warm and wonderful he felt. "Don't," he said, his breath warm against her cheek. "Come home with me."

Her body arched against his and she almost moaned with pleasure at the gentle contact. "I...I can't." Pausing, she moved slightly against him. "I should have left already."

Jake's mouth moved against her cheek, gently nipped at her ear. "You're a grown woman. You don't have a curfew. Stay with me."

There were a million reasons why she shouldn't.

Opening this door with him could only lead to heartache again.

His mouth moved down the slender column of her throat and Mallory's head slowly fell back to give him more access. It felt so good...so wonderful...so right...

"Mallory," he sighed as his arms slowly banded around her.

He continued to kiss her throat, her jaw, until his lips covered hers and then she was lost. There was no way to fight it and it didn't matter that this wasn't a good idea or how it would be that much harder to go back to her life in

New York, away from him. For tonight, she needed him. She needed this.

Jake said her name again—it was a breathless plea and Mallory responded with her own breathless "Yes."

Taking her by the hand, Jake carefully led her through the dark across the deck. He stopped to pick up her purse and handed it to her. "Text your mother so she knows you're safe," he said before making his way down to the pier.

Pausing, Mallory did as he requested before following him down. At the door to the boathouse, she stopped.

"Here," she said, reaching out for the door knob. "I want to stay here with you."

With nothing more than the light of the moon, she saw the confusion written on his face. "It would be a lot more comfortable up at my place."

She moved in close and placed soft kisses along his jaw. "Maybe later. But for right now, I want to be here. Please."

Reaching around her, Jake opened the door and slowly backed her inside. Once the door was closed behind them, Mallory refused to think of the past and didn't give the future a second thought. All she focused on was the here and now.

She kicked off her sandals as Jake peeled her blouse off. His hands immediately went to the button of her pants as hers snaked under his t-shirt and slid their way up over his chest. They kissed as they moved in the tiny space and they laughed as they bumped into things, but they never stopped moving—never stopped touching.

By the time she was naked and sprawled out on top of the oversized sofa she had always loved, and Jake was kneeling between her legs, she thought she'd go mad with want for him. She didn't want him to go slow, didn't want to spend too much time thinking about what they were doing.

Reaching up, she wrapped her hand around his nape and pulled him down for another searing kiss. He kicked his jeans off and Mallory helped slide his boxers down. And when they were skin to skin from head to toe, she let out a moan of pure pleasure.

He said her name as his mouth moved over her body.

She said his as she wrapped her legs around him.

And when their mouths and bodies finally joined together, there was no need for words any longer.

5

IT WAS after midnight and Jake sat back on the large sofa and watched Mallory scramble around getting dressed like she couldn't wait to leave.

Not the greatest moment for a man's ego...

When she was close enough for him to touch, he reached out and snagged her hand. "Hey," he said softly, "come back to the house with me."

She looked confused for a moment and then must have realized he meant *his* house. It was something they'd never done before–during that entire summer, they'd never spent an entire night together and all of their more intimate times had been here in the boathouse.

"I should probably go," she said, not looking at him.

Not letting go of her hand, he gave another gentle tug. "Why?"

Now she did look at him. "What do you mean why? It's late and we've..." She motioned toward the sofa. "You know. So...I should leave."

Ah...now he was getting it. Standing, he let the blanket that was covering him fall to the floor as he pulled her into his arms. "Here's the thing, Mal, there's no curfew and no one's waiting on us. I've got a house two minutes away that we can go to and crawl into bed and stay there all night." Placing a light kiss on the tip of her nose, Jake held his breath and waited for her to tell him why it wasn't a good idea.

And waited.

And waited.

Was it possible they were on the same page here?

Slowly, he stepped away and began his own search of his clothes and began getting dressed. They may have already had rounds one and two here in the boathouse, but the thought of finally having Mallory Westbrook in his bed for a whole night had him more than ready for round three.

Once he had his jeans on, Jake scooped up his shirt and found Mallory was still standing in the same spot. Okay, maybe she wasn't completely on the same page.

Yet.

Moving in close again, he kissed her cheek as his hands smoothed up and down her bare arms. "Please." It was one word and he thought it would be more powerful than a lengthy explanation of why she should come home with him.

"Okay."

That clearly worked.

Hand in hand, they left the boathouse and carefully made their way back up the pier and across the property to his house. Neither spoke other than for him to whisper for her to be careful as they navigated through the yard debris. Once they were in the house, Jake offered her something to drink which she readily accepted.

Now that she was here with him, he felt nervous and unsure of what he was supposed to do or say. The obvious move was to kiss her senseless and lead her into his bedroom, but...there was something about this moment that carried a lot of weight.

Reaching over to her, he took her purse from her hands and put it on the kitchen counter. Then he took one of her hands in his, led her into the living room and sat them both down on the couch. The entire back wall of the room was made of sliding glass doors so they had moonlight once again as their only light. When Jake looked at Mallory, he saw her studying him curiously.

"What?" he asked quietly.

"I thought you would have led us right to the bedroom," she said, just as quietly.

He shrugged. "It was my first instinct but I thought it might be nice to sit and talk for a bit. We haven't done that in a while."

She laughed softly. "Six years."

Then he couldn't help but laugh with her. "Give or take."

With a small smile on her face, Mallory moved in close and rested her head on his shoulder. "That summer seems like a lifetime ago sometimes."

"And others it feels like yesterday," he admitted. Kissing the top of her head, he whispered, "I've missed you."

Mallory sighed but didn't respond right away and Jake suddenly felt foolish for his admission. Then she put him out of his misery. "I've missed you too."

Relaxing, he wrapped one arm around her and held her close. "You know, if all you want to do is stay out here and talk all night, I'm fine with that." He paused. "Or if all you want to do is go inside and go to sleep, that's fine too." He kissed her head again.

"What if I want to go inside and crawl into bed and talk

to you there?" she asked, and there was a mixture of playfulness and insecurity to her voice that only Mallory could pull off.

"We could totally do that too."

She slowly moved out of his embrace and stood, holding out a hand to him. "I think I like option number three, but with a possibility of a fourth."

They walked down the short hallway to his room. When they were next to the bed, he kissed her–slowly, sweetly. There was no hurry. Jake simply enjoyed being able to kiss her again. It felt like the most natural thing in the world to undress each other again before sliding beneath the sheets. He wished he had known he was bringing her back here–he would have made more of an effort to make sure the place was cleaned up a bit more.

Mallory snuggled in close beside him and placed a kiss on his chest as she settled in.

"I want you to know," he said, "I didn't plan on this."

"Me either," she replied quietly, sleepily. "When I left Aunt Georgia's earlier, I really just needed to get away. I had gotten your text and when I showed it to my mother, she knew I was going to go to the house."

"I'm glad you did."

They were silent for a moment before Mallory thanked him.

"For what?"

"For getting the engineers out to the house. I know you must have had to pull some strings to make that happen, so...thank you."

"It's exactly what Zeke would have wanted me to do."

More silence.

"Jake?"

"Hmm?"

"This is nice."

He nodded. "It is."

"I'm only going to be here for two weeks," she said after a long pause. "I figured that would be enough time to come here and help with the cleanup and for the funeral."

Everything in him stilled. She was laying down the parameters for them and while he should have been thankful, right now he resented it. Six years ago they had been fine with a long-distance relationship. It hadn't been ideal, but they could have made it work. And even though just earlier today he was looking at spending time with Mallory as a way to get her out of his system once and for all, right now that logic seemed wrong.

And when she put it out there so bluntly?

He was more confused than ever.

It was hard not to be when he had Mallory naked and warm beside him in his bed. And that's when it hit him–if this was all they were going to have, two weeks, he was going to have to make the most of it so when she left this time, they wouldn't have any regrets.

She whispered his name again and Jake realized he was done talking. The clock on their time together started ticking only minutes ago and he didn't want to waste a second of the time they had.

Maneuvering them until he was stretched out on top of her, he leaned down and kissed her–this time deeply. And as she slowly wrapped herself around him–in a move he really loved–he gave himself over to whatever it was they were doing.

The sun was just coming up and the sound of an alarm

beeping woke her up. Mallory went to sit up, but Jake had one arm banded over her, keeping her still.

"Power's back," he murmured against her shoulder. He released her momentarily to shut off his alarm clock. "Everything else will calm down in a couple of minutes. All the electronics tend to make some sort of noise when they're starting up." He moved back up behind her–her back to his front–and it felt so good that she felt herself starting to doze again.

But her brain was already awake now.

"What time do you think it is? The clock is flashing midnight."

Behind her, he shrugged. "Five, maybe six." He yawned. "Too early to be up yet."

She knew what he meant. They hadn't slept more than a handful of hours and more than anything she wanted to be able to close her eyes and go back to sleep. But there was a lot to do today considering the power was back on and her mother was going to move back into Pops' place–and that meant she would too.

And there would be a lot to deal with.

When she went to move again, Jake's hold tightened. "Not yet, Mal," he said sleepily, kissing her shoulder again. "All night I dreamed about waking up and making love to you again as the sun came up."

His words affected her more than they should, she thought. They spent the night making love. How could he have been dreaming about doing it again?

"Jake..."

Effortlessly, he rolled her over until she was on her back looking up at him. "It's true. I dreamed of waking you up with sleepy kisses...like this."

And then he kissed her and it was slow and wet and just a little lazy but oh so good.

Lifting his head, he continued. "Then I was going to touch you...like this."

Mallory gasped and then sighed as his hand cupped her breast and played with her nipple. He lowered his head and just before he put his mouth where his hand was, he looked up at her and gave her the sexiest grin she had ever seen.

"And when we were done, I was going to make you breakfast." Then his mouth covered her breast and Mallory thought for sure there couldn't be a more perfect moment. She was lost in sensation and need. She raked her hands up into his hair and held on while he teased and tormented her. It seemed to just go on and on and on. They rolled around, giving and taking, until they were both weak and breathless.

It was hard to say how much time had passed because the alarm clock had been knocked to the floor at some point. But when Mallory forced herself to open her eyes, she caught Jake smiling at her.

"I hope you were thinking pancakes," she said with a wink.

Laughing, he pulled her in close and kissed her soundly before moving away and climbing from the bed. She admired his amazing body–fighting the urge to reach out and grab his ass one last time. Relaxing back against the pillows, she watched him get dressed before he told her he'd meet her in the kitchen.

She was so comfortable and feeling so damn lazy and all she wanted to do was stay in bed. Unfortunately, Mallory was too responsible to linger for long. Even though it was still early, she knew her mother was an early riser as well and would more than likely be anxious to get packed up and moved back home. Plus, Sam was due in today and there was going to be a lot going on. Sitting and playing house with Jake wasn't on the agenda.

Which was really a shame because she could smell the coffee brewing and knew she wouldn't mind waking up like this every day.

Sitting up, she looked out through the big wall of glass in front of her. Like the living room, one whole wall was made of sliding glass doors that led out to the deck, with an incredible view of the Sound. A view, she realized, that was better than the ones she ever had from her room over at Pops' place. With a long and languid stretch, Mallory allowed herself one last look at the scenery before she kicked the sheets off and got dressed.

In the kitchen, Jake kissed her even as he placed a cup of coffee into her hands.

Bless him...

"I do have the makings for pancakes," he said, turning to rummage through the pantry. "They're not as good as Gertie's or even the ones we used to get down at the diner, but they're definitely not bad." The boyish grin he gave her told her how nervous he was. "How many do you want?"

Laughing softly, Mallory walked up behind him and pulled him away from the food. "I was only kidding, Jake. I don't normally eat breakfast and really, I need to get going." Taking a sip of her coffee, she hummed with approval. "This is all I need."

"Mal, come on. You need more than coffee. I can scramble us a couple of eggs..."

Stopping him before he walked over to the refrigerator, she shook her head. "I'm serious," she said politely. "I'm sure my mother is more than ready to put a little distance between her and Aunt Georgia and I have her car. So essentially, she's stranded and I'm the reason she's still there."

"Only for another hour," he said with a wink before going back to the pantry. "Pancakes are quick!"

"Jake..."

Looking at her over his shoulder, he grinned. "It's either breakfast or a shower. Together. Your pick."

Sure breakfast was the most important meal of the day, but the thought of getting wet and soapy with Jake in a small shower certainly had its merits...

Nibbling on her lip, she weighed her options–shower, breakfast, or going to pick up her mother. Hmm...

Before she knew it, Jake was in front of her, taking the mug from her hands and placing it on the counter. Then, in a move she didn't see, he scooped her up in his arms and strode back down the hallway toward his bedroom.

Mallory was laughing hysterically because she couldn't believe they were seriously going to do this. "Jake!" she cried. "Oh my gosh, how can you even think about getting naked again?"

With a lecherous grin, he placed her on her feet next to the shower. "Making up for lost time," he said as he turned on the hot water.

Her laughter died in her throat as his words sank in. They were wonderful, wonderful words, but...

Reaching out, Mallory placed a hand on his arm. "You know I'm leaving again, right?" She thought certainly he was going to reconsider, turn off the water, and opt for breakfast.

But he didn't.

Instead, he leaned in close and kissed her. "I'm making the most of the time we have."

And it was hard to argue with that logic because...more than anything, she wanted to make the most of this time together as well.

"I know I should be thankful—and I am—but I am mentally exhausted." Those were the first words Susannah said once she and Mallory were alone in the car.

"It couldn't have been that bad..."

"My cousin is exhausting! She never sits still and she's always telling Beau and Mason what they need to be doing! Even when we lost power and were sitting in the dark, she was trying to tell them what to do!"

"Mom," Mallory said, laughing, "how is that possible? What could she possibly expect them to do in the dark?"

"Oh my goodness, it was all 'Beau, make sure you unplugged the unnecessary appliances' and 'Mason, I don't think you secured the boards over the windows well enough because I can hear them banging.' I'm telling you, it never stopped!"

"Ugh, no wonder Mason was murmuring about escaping!"

"That poor boy—well, man. Georgia is always on him for something, but Beau is no better. If I were Mason, I'd be looking for jobs overseas just to get away from them."

"You know he'll never do that. For all the ways we've joked about it over the years and even hearing you talk about the situation now, you know there's a part of him that wouldn't be able to handle living too far away from here and not getting praised all the time."

"I don't know," her mother argued lightly. "I think he's finally getting ready to snap. He seemed more annoyed than amused this week."

"It could just be all the other circumstances that are bothering him." She paused. "I know I bailed yesterday while all the arrangements for Pops were being made, but maybe this whole thing is bothering Mason more than he's letting on."

"Maybe, but I still think he's just biding his time until he can break free of Beau and Georgia's stranglehold on him. You know they weren't happy when he didn't get in to law school…"

"I think he purposely made sure that didn't happen."

"I wouldn't doubt it," Susannah said. "Still, they should be happy that he has a good job here with the town and is a decent young man, but they are always pushing for more!"

"It's so weird because they're not like that with Parker or Peyton. You would think it would have been the girls they were overprotective of."

But Susannah shook her head. "They're on the girls to marry well and be proper Southern belles. Which–FYI–I don't think is ever going to happen."

"Which part?"

"The proper Southern belle part," Susannah explained and immediately seemed flustered. "You know I love them both and I don't mean that in a bad way. Far from it. Those girls are strong and independent women and they aren't looking to be socialites. You ask me, they're looking at world domination more than anything else."

Mallory couldn't disagree. Her cousins were both fiercely independent and didn't like answering to anyone. And last she checked, neither were looking to get married or settle down any time soon.

"That must make Aunt Georgia crazy," she said with a laugh.

"I'm sure it does, but she doesn't even talk about it. Every conversation was about Mason!"

"That's a lot of pressure on him. Now I kind of feel bad for the years Sam and I made fun of him."

"Well, you should, but I understand why you did." They turned into the driveway at Pops' place and they both grew silent for a long moment. Just the sight of the house and the destruction all over the property was enough to distract them. It wasn't until they were parked that Susannah spoke again. "Speaking of Sam, did you talk to him at all today?"

"Mom, it's ten in the morning. I doubt Sam's even awake yet."

"That's not true. It's a Wednesday so it would be a workday for him. Plus, he promised he'd get on the road early so he could get here for lunchtime. I hope he really did that."

Mallory had her doubts but she wasn't going to voice them right now.

They climbed from the car and gathered the first round of luggage before trudging up the steps to the house. Neither spoke as they walked through the doors. The house smelled a bit musty and it was still far too quiet for Mallory's liking, but this was their reality right now.

"I'm going to open some windows," her mother said as she put her bags down at the foot of the stairs. "You do the upstairs and I'll do the ones down here."

They went off in their own directions and it was the perfect way to keep her mind off of the fact that it was only the two of them here now. Sure, Sam would arrive later on today and soon there would be construction crews here repairing the house, but right now it was too damn quiet. By the time they met back up at the bottom of the stairs, Mallory thought the silence was going to make her crazy. She was just about to comment on it when the doorbell rang.

"I'll get it," Susannah said, and Mallory went to walk

into the living room when she heard her mother talking to Jake.

Jake? What was he doing here?

When she'd left him earlier after a very sexy romp in the shower, they had agreed they were both going to be very busy for the next several days and they'd see each other when they could–no promises. So why was he already seeking her out?

Walking back to the entryway, she smiled. "Hey."

"Jake's already got a crew scheduled to come and work on the house!" her mother said excitedly. "Can you believe it? It's so fast!"

If Mallory wasn't mistaken, Jake actually blushed. "It's not a big deal, Susannah. You know Zeke would have already had people here. Coleman Construction is his baby and everyone was more than willing to come here and make the house a priority."

Sooo...he wasn't here for her. He was here on business.

For some reason that bothered her a little more than it should.

"Why don't you come into the kitchen and we can sit and talk about how this is all going to go?" Susannah suggested, leading the way. Jake followed after giving Mallory a wink and a smile. She still wasn't sure what she was supposed to do.

Her mother hadn't questioned her staying out last night–hadn't even mentioned the possibility of Mallory going to see Jake–and Mallory certainly hadn't volunteered that information. So now she was unsure if she was supposed to out them or simply let things be and play it cool.

"I am so not good at this sort of thing," she mumbled to herself as she made her way to the kitchen.

Jake had his tablet out and was sitting next to her mother at the table already. Mallory sat and joined them, listening as Jake explained all about the schedule of work that needed to be done.

"The first priority is tree removal," he was saying. "Considering half the trees in Magnolia Sound are down, it wasn't easy to convince a crew to come here. Their first priority is to get all the roadways cleared. But I happened to find a company willing to do it—they wanted to jack up the price on me, but I worked out a deal with them to give them first dibs on any and all upcoming Coleman projects that require tree removal."

"You can do that?" Mallory asked.

"I can," he confirmed. "Right now we're all moving forward as if nothing has changed. Zeke hasn't been involved in the day-to-day operations for a really long time, but in cases like this we always conferred with him first. Considering this is his home, I'm sure he would have agreed."

She nodded.

"Once all the trees are removed, we'll start on the house." He paused. "Actually, we've already tarped off the front of the house and I've hung plastic at the doorway to the damaged wing so the elements can't get through the main part of the house. We'll do our best to make sure the work on the addition doesn't interfere with you. We'll try to keep it as separate and unobtrusive as we can. The first step is to have a crew come in and remove the back deck."

Both she and her mother nodded.

Jake swiped the tablet screen and showed them a diagram of a deck. "This is what was already here," he explained. "I think that was completely functional and it was fine for all these years. However..." He swiped the screen again and showed another diagram. "This is something a little more...shall we say...modern. Zeke was all about keeping things simple, but I think we can all agree the house needs to be updated."

"God, yes," Susannah said.

Laughing, Jake turned the tablet toward her. "This will have built-in seating and flower boxes. We'll incorporate a pergola at the far corner so you can have some shading and we'll widen the stairs going down to the lawn."

"I love it!" Susannah cried. "But...okay, I know this is going to sound incredibly naïve of me, but...how are we paying for all of this, Jake? We haven't finished filing claims and we have no idea what's in Pops' will..."

"I know what you're saying, Susannah," he said calmly, "but I'll let you in on a little secret. Zeke has a home renovation account he's been putting money into for years. I'm the only one who knows about it and I'm the co-signer on the account."

Both Mallory and Susannah gasped in surprise. "What?!"

He nodded. "It's true. Zeke's always known this house needed some serious TLC. He just couldn't bear to watch it be done–unless it was an emergency or it wasn't too painful, like the summer you and I worked on his office and the boathouse," he said to Mallory.

"I remember a pipe bursting that summer too and he was sick over the renovations to the bathroom," she said with a small laugh. "He inspected the bathroom every day for about two weeks after it was done."

"He was still inspecting it last week," Susannah said with a sad smile. "We'd been talking a lot about doing work around here, but he never told me about this account."

"If I know Zeke, he wanted it to happen this way," Jake

said quietly. "Not that he wanted the house to be damaged, but he wanted to make sure the funds were here for you to do the work after he was gone." They were all silent for a moment. "He and I talked a lot about it–the house–whenever we got together. He would ask what I would do to the outside, what would I change here on the inside...but ultimately, it's going to be up to you, Susannah."

Both Mallory and Susannah looked at him oddly. "Well, we don't know that for sure, Jake," her mother said. "I'm sure the house is going to be either divided up between all of us or...I don't know, maybe Pops stated in his will what he wanted done with it." She paused. "I think we should stick to the basics for now to make the house stable and secure again. We won't get into anything design-wise until after the funeral."

Jake nodded, but he had a small smile on his face that told Mallory he knew more than he was saying, but she didn't want to mention it right now. Maybe later she'd ask him about it.

There was a loud noise outside and they all stood. "Looks like the tree removal crew is here," he said.

"Already?" Mallory asked, following him to the front door, her mother right behind her. "I didn't think you meant they would be starting today.

"No time like the present," he replied, stepping out onto the porch to greet the crew.

"Mom, are you okay with all of this? I mean...it's happening so fast."

Susannah nodded and waved to the man Jake was talking to before looking at Mallory. "This is the way it has to be and honestly, I'm relieved the cleanup is starting today. All the hanging limbs are making me nervous–like they could fall and do even more damage than we already have." She shook her head. "It's going to look strange around here once it's all cleared, but we have to think of it as a fresh start and keep on going."

It sounded logical, but there was a security in the way things were that Mallory was sad to see anything change. All the changes meant that Pops was truly gone and wouldn't be coming back. She swallowed hard and willed herself not to get emotional–after all, this was just tree removal they were dealing with right now.

Before she knew it, there was a team of workmen in the driveway with various large pieces of equipment and the cleanup immediately began. Jake jogged back up the front steps and came in through the front door smiling.

"Okay, they're going to get to work and it's going to be pretty loud out there for a while. They're going to remove the tree from the house first and then once that's taken care of, they're going to walk the property and start cleaning up. We need to figure on them being here for the next couple of days. Is that all right?"

Susannah nodded and laughed softly. "Are you kidding me? It's more than all right. The sooner things get cleared up, the better I'll feel. It's like I keep waiting for something else to fall on the house or on the property."

He nodded too. "I'm doing my best to make sure that doesn't happen." They walked back into the kitchen and sat down again. "So I need to ask you something," he began hesitantly, "but if you don't want to talk about it right now, that's okay."

"O-kay..."

"The funeral. Will you be having everyone back here or..."

Susannah's shoulders relaxed as she let out a breath. "Well, our first thought was that we wanted everyone to come back here, but even if there wasn't damage to the house and yard, we weren't sure we could make it happen. Beau talked to the funeral director and the pastor at Pops' church and we're going to have a big celebration service at the church, then go to the family cemetery for the burial, and then go back to the church for refreshments. The church is going to set up one of their big tents for us and Georgia's organizing the caterer for it." She paused again. "I think we may have the family come back here afterwards, but that's not set in stone yet. Georgia offered to host the family since their property is in good shape."

"Probably because she had Mason out there with a chainsaw at the crack of dawn," Mallory murmured and then smiled when both her mother and Jake laughed.

"Well, that's part of it," her mother confirmed, "but honestly, if there were a way to have everyone here, I think Pops would have preferred that. I just don't think we can make it happen in such a short timeframe."

"I wish I could tell you otherwise, but...I can't," Jake said sadly.

"It's okay, Jake. Really," Susannah replied. "This entire situation isn't the way any of us envisioned it would be and we're making do. I'm just so glad you're able to help out so much and know exactly what to do where this mess is concerned with the house. Other than the insurance claims, I wasn't sure how to even begin, so...thank you." Before she could say anything else, her cell phone rang and she looked at the screen and smiled. "It's Sam. Will you both excuse me?" She walked out of the room, leaving Jake and Mallory alone.

Jake looked over his shoulder before reaching out and taking one of Mallory's hands in his. "Hey."

She could feel herself blush. "Hey."

"You doing okay with all this? It's going to look a lot worse before it looks better."

"I know," she said softly, stroking her thumb over his knuckles. "Thank you for doing all of this. There's just so much to do and I appreciate you taking the time to help out like this."

He mimicked her actions. "He was my friend, too, Mal. By doing all of this...well...it's my way of helping Zeke out."

She nodded.

"I really want to kiss you right now," he said, his voice low and gruff and so damn sexy that she actually shivered a little.

"Then why don't you?" she whispered.

"I wasn't sure if you told your mother or anyone about where you spent the night last night. I didn't want to make assumptions."

It was nice how he was being considerate but she kind of hated it too–hated how they even had to think of these things. Although, she hadn't really wanted to tell her mother, or anyone else for that matter, where she spent last night, because it wasn't anyone's business. What she did last night was between the two of them.

"The fact that you're not saying anything tells me I was right," he said and maybe it was her imagination, but he sounded a little disappointed.

"I just don't think what we're doing concerns anyone," she argued lightly.

"Right." He slowly pulled his hand away and went to stand up.

"Hey, what's going on?" she asked. Could he seriously be upset because she didn't announce to her family that they'd spent the night together?

"I need to get going," he said, picking up his tablet and

phone. "I've got a lot of crews going back to work today, so..."

She let him go all of three steps before reaching out and grabbing his arm. When he turned to her, Mallory could see the frustration there on his face. It was on the tip of her tongue to lash out and remind him how they'd talked only a few hours ago about making no promises or any demands on each other, but she didn't see the point. Instead, she moved in close and kissed him with all of her own pent-up frustration. It was all wild heat and need and she was just about to wrap herself fully around him when she heard her mother clear her throat.

"I don't care where this goes, but I've got too much on my plate to handle any more drama," Susannah said before walking away.

And all Jake and Mallory could do was laugh.

6

MALLORY SAT with her eyes facing forward, refusing to look at the flower-covered casket. She couldn't. Her brother sat beside her holding her hand tightly while her cousin Peyton sat on her right side, holding her other hand. She thought she was prepared for this—had been telling herself for days that she could handle it—but once she sat down and Pastor Steve started speaking about Pops and his life, she crumbled.

"I look around this room and I see how many lives Ezekiel Coleman touched. How many here today can share a story of a time when Ezekiel took the time to talk with them? Or gave them business advice? Or even just shared a story about what life was like here in Magnolia Sound way back when?" the pastor asked and Mallory knew everyone in the church was nodding.

"As I drove here today and I saw all of the destruction Hurricane Amelia caused, it occurred to me that it's not just the structures that have been changed, but the lives of everyone here—in this town and in this room. But most of all, what struck me was how when everything is fixed and everything is rebuilt, it will be a new beginning. We will be a new town," he said and then paused. "But we will be a new town that Ezekiel Coleman will never see. Over the course of his life, he watched this town grow from nothing – nothing but the land that was here – and then helped it transform into a place we all call home. I believe there's a little bit of him in every home and every business here in Magnolia Sound. He gave so much to so many and for so long that his legacy and his memory will live on."

Tears streamed down Mallory's cheeks but she didn't want to let go of Sam or Peyton to wipe them away. So many people got up to speak after the pastor stepped down that Mallory lost track. By the time they were all standing and getting ready to head out of the church, she felt completely exhausted.

Slowly they followed the casket down the long church aisle and then stood on the steps as it was loaded into the hearse. The entire time, she continued to hold her brother's hand. She and Sam were as close as any twins could be, and even though they didn't get to see each other nearly enough, she was beyond grateful that he was here beside her now.

"How you holding up?" he leaned down and asked. They were surrounded by so many people and more than anything, Mallory couldn't wait to get into the car and have a little time to pull herself together.

"I want to just go home and curl up in bed for a little while," she replied, leaning her head on his shoulder.

Together they made their way down the steps and Sam released her hand long enough to let Mallory and their mother climb into the waiting limousine. Once they were settled, Sam joined them and immediately took her hand back in his again before reaching and taking his mother's hand in his other one. They were a tight little family unit and it had been a long time since they were alone like this.

"You doing okay, Mom?" Sam asked.

Beside him, Susannah sighed. "It made me feel good to see how many people came out to pay their respects and to hear all those testimonies to all he had done in his life." She sniffled and wiped at her eyes. "He was always so much larger than life and it feels weird that we're never going to see him again."

That reality had been settling in more and more each day and yet it still hurt.

The funeral procession made its way through town, passing all of the places that had been important to Pops – on the main street, the offices of Coleman Construction, Café Magnolia, The Dream Bean Coffee Shop. After several turns, they drove by the warehouse that held all of the landscaping equipment for Coleman Landscaping which was next to the offices of the Magnolia Marina. As the long line of cars wove its way around, the final stop was to drive by the plantation-style home where Pops lived for almost his entire life. It broke Mallory's heart to know he'd never walk through those doors again. Her heart squeezed tight as it hit her how they were now heading to his final resting place.

They were going to go to the cemetery and say their final goodbyes. Then they were supposed to go and celebrate Pops' life back at the church before heading back to his house to have a private family memorial.

That in and of itself was causing some added drama to the day. Here they were in one limo, Aunt Georgia, Uncle Beau, Mason, Parker, and Peyton were following in another limo, and in a third were her cousins Garret, Jackson, and Austin along with their mother, Grace. The only one missing was her uncle Cash. He was Susannah and Georgia's cousin and no one had seen or heard from him in years–including his wife and kids. The family lawyer had said he'd spoken to him, but he was a no-show at the wake last night and at the church today. And if Mallory had to guess, she'd say he'd be a no-show for all of it.

Aunt Georgia had argued that Aunt Grace and the boys didn't need a limo of their own or to be included in the family get-together later today, but Susannah held firm and now everyone was tense. It seemed that not even a funeral could force people to get along and be nice.

Seriously, she was exhausted and over all of this and just wanted to be alone for a little while.

Somewhere in all the chaos, Mallory had lost sight of Jake. She'd seen him come into the church and he was sitting several rows behind her, but once they exited, she didn't know where he'd went. She wanted to ask him to ride to the cemetery with her and her family, but never got the chance. After their kiss-at the house the other day, they hadn't seen much of each other. Between the work on the house and property, Sam coming home, planning the funeral...there was always something going on. Last night she had wanted to just say to hell with all the responsibilities and go over and see him, but when she was halfway across the yard she saw that his house was dark. Dejectedly, she'd gone back home and went to bed early.

She missed him.

More than she should, considering this was temporary.

But her time here in Magnolia was halfway over and... she wasn't nearly ready to say goodbye to him.

She wasn't sure if she ever would be.

Mallory looked up as the car slowed down and saw they

were turning into the cemetery already. She let out a shaky breath and Sam squeezed her hand.

I can do this, she said to herself, but she wasn't really sure. She knew she had to, but it was going to take every ounce of strength she had to make it happen.

There were certain things that made Jake think of Mallory.

One was summer days. They always reminded him of her because that was their time–even though they had only dated for one summer. Another was sunset. How many times had he come outside at the end of a long day and seen her standing out on the party deck of the boathouse watching the sunset?

So many.

Like now.

It had been an emotionally grueling day and while part of him wanted to walk across the yard and go have a strong drink alone in his house, the sight of her standing all alone up there was too much to ignore.

They had seen each other all day but they were never alone. He'd longed to go over and wrap his arms around her and hold her and make sure she was all right, but her brother had been like some sort of militant guard by her side all damn day. He and Sam never quite reconnected after the breakup. Naturally, Sam sided with Mallory and he didn't fault him that, but...he missed his friend and wished they could move forward–especially now that he and Mallory were okay.

Quietly he made his way down to the pier and was surprised no one else was outside. True, the deck was gone and it took a little more of an effort to get back here, but it wasn't impossible. And he would have thought if Sam wasn't with Mallory that maybe Parker and Peyton would be.

But now he was glad they weren't.

When he was finally there and climbing up the steps to get to her, he wondered if he was making a mistake. Maybe–like him–she had come out here to be alone. He paused on the second to last step and considered turning around. She hadn't spotted him yet, so...

Then she did. The sad smile on her face was all it took for him to stop second-guessing himself and go to her. Wordlessly, he walked over and took her in his arms. Part of him expected her to cry–everything in her expression told him she might–but she didn't and he was proud of her. Knowing how much of a toll the day had taken on him, no doubt it was doubly hard on her.

The sun continued its descent and they stayed locked in each other's embrace until it was almost dark. Finally, Mallory spoke.

"I dreaded this day so much and I just want it to be over."

"I know what you mean," he replied softly, placing a kiss on her forehead. She shivered slightly and he held her tighter. The September nights were starting to grow cooler and he knew her sleeveless dress wasn't going to keep her warm. Slipping his suit jacket off, Jake placed it over her shoulders before pulling her in close again.

"Thank you."

It was probably the wrong time to ask, but he couldn't seem to stop the words from coming out of his mouth. "Want to come home with me for a little while?"

Pulling back, Mallory blinked up at him. He was

waiting for her refusal–expecting it–but as usual, she surprised him. "I'd like that."

They turned and hadn't gone more than a few steps when Sam appeared at the top of the steps. "There you are, Mal. Everyone's looking for you."

The way she angled away from Jake was probably only noticeable to him, but it annoyed him nonetheless. "Why?" she asked.

Sam shrugged. "Aunt Grace and the guys left already and everyone else was getting ready to go and wanted to say goodbye, I guess." He eyed Jake suspiciously before returning his attention to his sister. "You know Peyton and Parker will want to talk to you before they go."

Off in the distance, they all turned at the sound of car doors slamming shut. A minute later, it wasn't hard to see the headlights and taillights as the car pulled away.

"So much for wanting to say goodbye," she murmured.

The way he saw it, they could all stand here awkwardly, or he could just put it out there what they were already planning. "We were just going to hang out over at my place," he said, placing his arm around Mallory. Jake had to admit, he almost pulled it back when Sam's expression turned a little fierce. "Why don't you join us?" he blurted out and almost laughed at both Sam and Mallory's confused expressions.

"Um..." Sam said, looking away.

"Oh, uh...sure," Mallory said to her brother. "You should come and hang out for a bit. It could be fun."

None of this was going quite the way Jake had planned, but if getting to hang out with Mallory meant Sam coming along, he'd deal with it.

"Sure," Sam eventually said. "I'll text Mom and let her know where we are."

They all made their way down from the deck, up the pier, and across the yard in relative silence. Once they were inside Jake's house, he gave Sam a beer, grabbed one for himself, and looked to Mallory. "What would you like?"

"I'm going to be the lame one and ask if you have any tea," she said shyly. "Hot or cold, doesn't matter."

Jake reached into the refrigerator, pulled out a bottle of sweet tea and handed it to her before motioning them all to the living room. He had to admit, he was relieved when Mallory sat close beside him while Sam sat across the room in the large recliner. Clearing his throat, Jake asked, "So how've you been, Sam? It's been a while."

Clearly, Sam couldn't be fooled. He eyed the two of them before sagging back against the cushions. "You two are back together, huh?"

This time Jake knew to let Mallory speak first. He glanced at her and held his breath while he waited for her response.

"I wouldn't say back together," she said slowly, kicking her shoes off and curling her legs up beside her. "But...we're spending time together while I'm here."

With a curt nod, Sam took a pull of his beer. "And when do you go home?"

"Next weekend. Sunday, actually. I need to be back at work on Monday." She sighed and took a sip of her tea. "I already got grief for taking two weeks off on such short notice, and with the new position..."

"There was a death in the family," Sam snapped. "How much advanced notice did they think you could give?"

"I know, I know...and considering I hardly ever take time off, you'd think they'd be a little more understanding. Still, I think they're just a little lost without me. I'm always there and I was ready to lead up a new team for an upcoming project so...I really should touch base with my boss and make sure everything is okay."

Jake frowned as he listened to the conversation and felt a little out of the loop. Mallory was talking about how much she liked her job and she sounded very enthusiastic about it. Leaning back, he took a pull of his own beer and wondered what a typical day was like for her. Was she one of those big city career women in a power suit or did she work in a more casual atmosphere?

"Don't you have any extra time coming to you?" Sam asked. "I mean, it's not going to solve anything because you're eventually going to go back, but with all the storm damage, the funeral, and we still have the reading of the will on Wednesday, I just think you should take more time."

"For what?" she asked.

"You don't know what we're going to find out in the will, right? For all you know, Pops left you a small fortune and...and...you can quit your job!" Sam saluted her with his bottle and took another drink. "How freaking cool would that be?"

Jake laughed softly and noticed Mallory did too. "It would definitely be cool, but I'm not counting on it," she replied logically. "That's not the kind of thing he would've done. We all know he had a lot of money and he invested it in a lot of different ways, but I don't think he had the kind of money that would mean all of his grandchildren and great-grandchildren could all retire and never work again."

But Sam shook his head. "That's not what I meant. We all know you were his favorite. For all you know, he left you everything."

Her blue eyes went wide and she looked at Jake incredulously before looking at her brother. "Are you crazy? How much have you had to drink today?"

"Not nearly enough," he said, finishing off his beer. "Look, maybe I'm way off base here, but you can't deny that you and Pops were closer than any of us ever were. Everyone knows it."

"They do not," she denied. "Stop it. You're crazy."

Sam just laughed and looked at Jake. "Tell her. You know you spent a lot of time with the old man. You tell her how much time he spent with any of our cousins."

When Mallory turned to look at him, Jake knew he looked more than a little panicked. The truth was, Sam was right. None of Zeke's grandchildren or great-grandchildren spent the kind of time with him the way Mallory did and, on top of that, Zeke never talked about anyone else the way he did with Mallory. Still...he was no expert on the matter.

"You think Sam's crazy too, right?" she prompted.

Letting out a long breath, he glanced at Sam and saw him nod before looking back at Mallory. "He's right, Mal. You and Zeke were like...nothing else I've ever seen," he said softly, watching as her expression went a little sad. Reaching out, he took one of her hands in his. "You were the one he talked about the most, the one he bragged most about, and...you were the only one who seemed to spend any quality time with him." When he saw tears welling in her eyes, he knew he needed to lighten the mood. "Not that I think he's leaving you millions or anything, but I wouldn't be surprised if he left you a little something extra."

She wiped away a stray tear and shook her head. "You guys are the worst!" she cried and then laughed. "I still think you're both crazy and I don't care what Pops left me or if he left me anything at all!"

Sam stood and walked into the kitchen to help himself to another beer. When he came back, he grinned at his sister. "We'll see if you're still saying that after he leaves you something fantastic." He was about to say more but his phone beeped with an incoming text. Frowning, he sat down and quickly typed something out.

"Everything okay?" Mallory asked.

"Mason wants to go hang out. He said he needs to get out of the house and he already used me as his excuse."

"Mason knows he's a grown man, right?" Jake asked, chuckling. "Why does he need an excuse to go out?"

"Please, you've met his parents, right?" Sam asked, responding to yet another text. "As much as he annoys the shit out of me, it's mostly because of his folks." He shrugged. "He seemed a lot more tolerable today so maybe going out with him won't be the worst thing in the world."

"But we were already hanging out," Mallory reminded him and the look Sam gave her bordered on hysterical. "What? What's so funny?"

"We all know I'm the third wheel here and the two of you would like nothing more than to be alone, so...I'm leaving," he said, walking back into the kitchen to put the beer back in the refrigerator. "I'm gonna go home and tell Mom what the plan is–I'm going out to be a good cousin, while you're here doing...I don't know...Jake." He winked. "You two have fun!"

Jake knew he didn't let out a breath until the back door closed and he saw Sam walk down the deck stairs from the living room window. "Well...that was...awkward."

"Just a little," Mallory agreed. "Ugh...why is my brother such a dork?"

Laughing, Jake shifted them until her head was on his shoulder. "I wouldn't call him a dork, he's just a little..."

"He's a dork. Trust me. We're twins and I'm allowed to say it." She shook her head. "He's going to be snarky about this until he leaves."

"About what?"

"You and me. Us. The fact that he knows what we're doing." She groaned. "Now, every time I mention seeing you or doing something, he's going to make some sort of doofus comment about how I'm doing *you*. I'm telling you, he's the worst."

But Jake couldn't help but laugh. He didn't have any siblings so he didn't understand the dynamics, but from where he was sitting, it was all pretty comical. The fact that they each other and had such obvious affection for each other was a pretty amazing thing. Maybe it was because they were twins or something. All he knew was that he hadn't met many siblings with the kind of relationship Sam and Mallory had.

Plus, he liked knowing Sam looked out for her when he couldn't.

And that one single thought had him going still.

This wasn't going anywhere–this was about passing the time and getting her out of his system. He wasn't supposed to be thinking about his feelings or hers. This was temporary. They both saw the end before they started up again, so why was he suddenly feeling concerned about how Mallory was going to be when he wasn't around?

"Jake?" she asked softly, looking up at him. "You okay?"

He nodded. Right now, he didn't want to talk. Hell, he didn't want to think either. All he wanted was to feel–feel Mallory's body against his. Feel her skin under his hands. Feel her breath mingling with his.

Standing, he gently tugged her to her feet before plunging his hands into her hair and giving her a searing kiss. If she was surprised by the sudden change of events, she didn't show it. If anything, she kissed him back with equal abandon.

So good, he thought. Kissing Mallory was always so damn good...

When he had invited her to come home with him earlier–before Sam showed up–Jake envisioned them coming in and talking and maybe sharing some lazy kisses before he seduced her into staying the night. But as Mallory pressed up against him and purred, he was pretty sure nothing was going to be slow and lazy, and that he was the one being seduced.

And he loved every minute of it.

Without breaking the kiss, they maneuvered across the room and down the hall, stopping once so he could back her against the wall and grind against her. She tore her lips from his and sighed his name like a plea. Reaching down, Jake lifted her until her legs wrapped around his waist and it took every bit of self-control he possessed not to take her right then and there. Her dress was bunched up at her waist and the barely-there panties would be gone with only the slightest of tugs...

"Bed," he growled against her throat even as he continued to rub against her. "I want you in my bed."

"Then take me there," she said breathlessly.

Easier said than done, he thought, forcing himself to walk the last ten feet to his room. At the side of the bed, he simply let himself fall and kept Mallory in his arms. They laughed and rolled until they were comfortable and then he sank back into the kiss.

Mallory tugged at his shirt and once she had it pulled free of his trousers, her nails scraped up his back and it gave him chills. Sitting up quickly, he ripped the shirt off–buttons flying in every direction.

"Wow," she panted. "That was incredibly sexy."

"Oh, yeah?" he asked, his own breath coming out

roughly. "How do you feel about this?" His hand snaked under her dress and he tugged her tiny panties off–the sound of the fabric ripping seemed insanely loud in the room.

"Oh!" she cried as her hips bucked off the bed. Jake knew what she wanted and he was more than happy to give it to her. In a flash her dress was off. He peeled her bra off with his teeth as she writhed beneath him. "Jake..."

Once he had her completely naked, his self-control completely vanished. His mouth and hands were everywhere. While he licked and suckled at her breasts, his hand was ruthlessly teasing her between her legs. Watching Mallory lose control was one of his favorite pastimes and as he urged her on, he knew it would always be this way. She cried out his name again and again and again and each time it ratcheted his own arousal up more and more.

He hated to move away from her even for a second, but he still had half of his own clothes to discard. Mallory reached for him as he moved away and he smoothed a hand across her stomach. "Soon," he whispered. "I'm not going anywhere."

"Hurry..."

Suddenly he felt like he was all thumbs. His belt wouldn't come off, then he seemed to get tangled up in the pants legs as he tried to kick them off. By the time he was naked, Mallory pushed him onto his back and straddled him.

And what a glorious sight it was.

She smiled down at him right before she leaned down to kiss him. Anchoring his hand in her hair, he knew neither of them were going to get any sleep tonight.

And neither of them seemed to care.

They were sipping coffee the next morning out on the back deck and all Jake could think of was how it felt damn-near perfect. It was a beautiful day already–the temperatures were cool and he was a little sore and tired from the night, but he was sitting next to the most beautiful girl in the world. Everything was as it should be.

Except...

It was like the first night he saw her out on the pier. Right now everything seemed ideal, but it was just a mirage–there was no happy ending for them. At least...he didn't think there was.

Glancing over at Mallory, he saw the look of total peace on her face. She was smiling up at the sky as she cradled her coffee mug in her hands. She was wearing one of his shirts and her bare legs were crossed. She looked sexy as hell.

Down boy...

What would it be like to wake up like this every day? To know he could start his day looking at her face and go to sleep every night with her in his arms? Six years ago, he wasn't ready for that reality. There were too many things he wanted to do with his life and Mallory had plans of her own as well. The timing wasn't right for either of them and now that emotions weren't running quite so high, he knew they could both agree on that. While it was true he hadn't handled things in the best of ways–had insulted her and deliberately pushed her away–but it was for the best at the time.

Now? Well, now it was a completely different story and Jake sat there wondering why they were holding themselves to their past when there was a possibility of a future for them.

Of course, he was only thinking for himself. He had no idea what Mallory was thinking where the two of them were concerned.

Clearing his throat, he figured there was no time like the present to feel her out on the subject. "So...last night, you and Sam talked about your job," he began casually. "Sounds like big things are happening for you there."

Slowly, she shifted in her chair and looked over at him, her peaceful smile still in place. "They are," she replied. "I always envisioned myself working on exciting new programs and being at different companies all the time, but what it turned into was me being stuck at the same places for long periods of time working on systems that aren't particularly challenging and trying to convince people to upgrade. It was mentally exhausting and my hours were killer." She paused. "But all that is finally behind me because I got a promotion and I'm going to have a lot more freedom while working fewer hours."

He nodded and took a sip of his coffee. "Sounds great."

Hopefully he didn't sound as disgruntled as he felt.

"I hope it will be. I love technology and learning about all the new systems and apps..." She paused and sighed. "It was a lot more taxing than I thought it would be. I'm hopeful this new position will still be challenging even if it means I'm not out in the field as much." Another pause. "Either way, it is what it is. This is the career I chose–the one I got my degree in–so..."

"Mal, you're allowed to do something other than what your college diploma says," he argued lightly. "I mean...not that you're even suggesting that, but...still..."

"I know, and for a while I considered it–especially if I didn't get this promotion, but...it would make me feel like a quitter or like I couldn't handle the job."

"No one's saying that." But part of him felt guilty because there was a time when he was the one accusing her of running away from her problems rather than dealing with them.

Probably not the time to remind her of that.

She gave him a small smile but turned her attention back to her coffee and looking out at the Sound.

Then he figured he'd throw something else out there for her to think about.

"You used to talk a lot about living here in Magnolia," he said carefully, making sure he was looking out at the water and not at her. "I remember you telling me how you used to beg your mom to move here. Well, she's here now and you could be too."

Jake could feel her eyes on him and he fought the urge to look back at her. His heart was hammering like wild in his chest because he knew what he was trying to say without saying it. He didn't want to spook or scare her, but this was something he wanted her to start considering.

"I can't just pick up and move, Jake. I have a job and a home and..."

Now he did look. "People change jobs and move all the time, Mal," he countered.

She didn't immediately respond, but he did notice that her expression was no longer sweet and relaxed.

Maybe he shouldn't have brought this up yet.

"Why are you doing this?" she asked quietly, still not looking at him. "I mean, why now?"

Frowning, he looked at her in confusion. "What do you mean?"

"We talked about this..."

"Briefly," he interrupted.

A loud sigh was her immediate response. "You know

what I mean, Jake." Now she did look at him and the look on her face made him ache. "We said no promises, no making demands on each other. That was only a few days ago and now..." Another sigh. "You're just thinking like this because of the sex."

"No!" he said adamantly. "No, it's not that."

"It's okay," she replied calmly. "Right now is...it's kind of like our summer. It's temporary, but it's easy to get caught up in. Can't we just enjoy the week?"

"Mallory, this is nothing like our summer..."

Only...it was.

Before she could argue, he had more to say. "The timing back then sucked. We knew we were on borrowed time and were looking at a long-distance relationship if we wanted to keep seeing each other."

She gave him a very neutral look.

And he didn't take it as a good sign.

"A lot has changed since then. We're both older..."

"And more mature," she added with a hint of sarcasm that he totally knew wasn't a good sign.

"Yes, we're *both* more mature," he corrected. "I think we have something good here, Mallory, and it's not just about the sex."

"But it helps," she murmured.

With a sigh, he hung his head. This was not going the way he had hoped. And one of the things he learned with his maturity, was when to fight and when to pull back.

This was definitely a situation where he needed to pull back.

Doing his best to seem like all was right with his world, Jake shrugged. "It was just an idea. No big deal."

She didn't look like she believed him but luckily she didn't argue either. And that was fine with him. Let her think what she wanted because he had one week to prove her wrong. He was going to remind her of all the ways they worked and made sense, and how there was a time when they were in love.

He was going to remind her of it all. And as he took a sip of his own coffee, he hid a smug smile.

Let the wooing begin.

7

SOMETHING WAS UP.

Mallory couldn't quite put her finger on it, but the next day as she went about her business, everything seemed different.

Or maybe she was just paranoid.

No matter how much she tried to downplay her conversation with Jake, the bottom line was that she couldn't stop thinking about it. He wanted her to stay? Was it just because he was concerned about her as a friend–or a friend with benefits? She immediately pushed that option aside because it seemed crazy. Was he looking to pick up where they left off so many years ago? And was it crazy how just the thought of that had her heart beating a bit faster?

And all that aside, it was everything else around her that left her confused.

When she got back from Jake's yesterday morning, she ran into Sam who was acting all squirrelly. She'd asked him if everything was okay, but he avoided giving her a direct answer.

Which was an answer in and of itself, whether he realized it or not.

Knowing him, he and Mason had gotten into some kind of trouble on their night out and were hoping no one found out about it.

They would.

This was a small town and nothing stayed secret for long. Hell, it seemed like almost everyone in town who came to Pops' funeral remembered something Mallory had said or done over one summer or another. Granted, most of the things they remembered were very sweet, but where her brother was concerned, he seemed to attract trouble simply by being himself. He dated half the girls in town and got rowdy with half the boys, so...there was no doubt that the town would know about anything he and Mason did.

Then, there was Susannah. Ever since the call about Pops came, they both knew Mallory was only going to be here for two weeks. But suddenly, her mother was hinting at things she wanted the two of them to do together after she was supposed to go home. She mentioned that things were so hectic because of the cleanup and the funeral so it would be nice to simply go to lunch together, but it seemed more like an excuse. Something about it all just felt like there was more pressure than usual, particularly when she mentioned going furniture shopping to replace the items destroyed in the storm and needing help with updating the space.

It was something the two of them had often talked about – updating Pops' house – and now here was the opportunity and Mallory was going to miss it.

"Oh, and I made an appointment with Barb over at Barb's Beach Buys to see what she has in stock, too. You know she always has the best pieces," her mother had added, like adding insult to injury because that specific place was Mallory's favorite.

Coincidence? Maybe.

But then how could she explain Parker and Peyton suddenly talking about all the things they could do together if Mallory moved back?

"Oh, my gosh!" Parker had cried excitedly. "How cool would it be get together for brunch every Saturday? You know, like they did on *Sex and the City*?"

"Or we could go to Polish Me Pretty and get our nails done!" Peyton suggested. "I swear, Lynne and her girls do the best job on my manicure!" She held up her hands and wiggled her fingers for proof. "Plus, they serve wine! I get some of the juiciest town gossip while I'm there."

"I don't know," Parker countered. "I prefer the pedicure I get at Glitter Girls." She giggled. "Besides, it's very entertaining to listen to Julie talk about her man of the month!"

Mallory had frowned at that. "Isn't Julie like..."

"She's in her sixties!" Parker said, still giggling. "I think she has the hottest dating life in town!"

And she had to admit, the thought of having the kind of girly days her cousins were talking about was seriously appealing. It had been a long time since she'd done anything like that and it was something they had done during her summers here once they were all old enough. Wouldn't it be nice to make more of those memories with her family? Had Jake somehow gotten some sort of secret message out to her family that he had talked to her about this?

Or...

Her heart sank. What if her family had talked to Jake and asked him to talk to her about moving back? What if this wasn't about Jake wanting her here full time, but her family?

Mallory was sitting in Pops' office when Sam came walking in the front door. "Hey!" she called out and watched him almost trip. Snickering, she waved him into the room. "Where were you this afternoon?"

"Out."

She rolled her eyes. "Can you sit down for a minute? I need to ask you something." And something in her tone must have made him realize she was serious because he didn't question her or give her a snarky comeback. He simply sat down.

"What's up?"

Sighing, she rested her arms on the massive mahogany desk. "Did you say anything to anyone about me quitting my job and moving here?"

Sam's eyes went wide. "Wait, you're thinking about it?"

"Yes, I mean...no!" She growled with frustration. "I mean ever since you brought it up in that ridiculous conversation at Jake's the other night, it seems like everyone is talking to me about moving here."

A snort of laughter was his first response. "Mal, what did you expect? You've talked about it our whole lives and now you're here and...I don't know...it seems like the next logical step for you."

She eyed him warily. "Really?"

"Sure," he nodded. "We all know the only thing holding you to Long Island is your job. And if I had to guess, I'd say there wasn't any*one* really tying you there either. You're not dating anyone, are you?"

Now she looked at him incredulously. "Would I be... you know...with Jake if I was?"

He laughed again. "I guess not. For all I know you're both just messing around as a way to pass the time. You're not serious about him again, are you?"

And for the first time in a long time, she couldn't look directly at her brother because she knew he'd see through any lie she tried to tell right now.

"Mal?"

Groaning, she face-planted on the desk. "I don't know, okay?" Then she straightened and looked at him. "Maybe I am, maybe I'm not...it's a lot to think about right now!"

Raking a hand through his sandy brown hair, Sam slouched down in his chair and let out a long breath. "Look, can I be honest with you?"

She nodded. "Please."

Shifting, Sam leaned forward and rested his elbows on his knees. "I know you crushed hard on Jake for years before the two of you even got together," he began. "And once you two hooked up, I tried to see it as a good thing."

"But...?"

"But, at the time, I didn't think you were mature enough to be dating an older guy, and it pissed me off that Jake would even consider getting involved with you."

"Why?"

"Because...okay, you can't get mad at me for this, but... he kind of had a reputation around here. He was a guy who dated a lot of girls and never went on more than three dates with one."

"How do you even know that?"

"Because we spent every summer here, Mal! I hung out with him! I hung out with his friends! People talk! Hell, he was kind of my idol!"

"Why didn't you say anything back then?" she demanded, feeling majorly annoyed and betrayed how they were just now having this conversation.

"It wouldn't have mattered what I said. You were determined to go after Jake and I figured it would last the summer–if even that long–and then you'd go your way and he'd go his." He sighed. "The fact that the two of you are picking up where you left off is a little...well...it's a little surprising to me."

"Why? Because someone like Jake couldn't possibly still be interested in someone like me?" she asked and willed herself not to pout.

Now it was Sam's turn to roll his eyes. "No, Mal, that's not what I'm saying." He huffed with annoyance. "I remember how crushed you were when the two of you broke up. Then I remember how much you used to dread coming here to visit Pops until you realized Jake wasn't coming home for his summer breaks. And then, when he finally was back, you stopped coming here. You missed our annual visit and..."

"Okay, okay, I get it," she quickly interrupted–not wanting the reminder of how she didn't come this summer and missed her chance to see her great-grandfather one last time.

"I thought you had moved on–that you both had. So I don't know if this is just proximity or you're scratching an itch..."

"Sam..."

"Whatever it is, I'm not judging, okay? I just don't want you to get hurt," he said firmly. "I still have issues with Jake because of the way things went down with the two of you and until he proves that he's changed..." He shrugged. "I'm still going to have issues with him. I can't help it."

And that's what brothers were supposed to say and do, right? Mallory loved that Sam was being so protective of her, but she didn't want Sam to be at odds with Jake. They had been friends long before she came between them. "He has changed," she said softly. "We both have. I don't know what we're doing. I thought this was just a…a…temporary fling, but…"

"But…?"

"Yesterday morning, he made me feel like he wanted me to stay. Like really stay. Permanently. And not just because Mom's here, but…for us. Me and him."

"And you don't believe him?"

"I'm afraid to," she admitted and hated how pathetic she sounded. "The last time, I was all in. I was in love and wanted a future and thought that was where we were heading. I was the one to say 'I love you,' and he never really said it back. I don't want to go there again. I don't want to put my time and energy and…heart into a relationship that isn't going to go anywhere."

He nodded.

"I'm older now and…and I'd like to start thinking about my future–about settling down and getting married and having kids. I know that doesn't mean it's going to happen right now or that I need it to happen right now. But if I'm going to get involved in a committed relationship, I need to know that person is thinking along those lines too."

"And you don't think Jake is?"

"That's just it. I don't know."

"You could try asking." Sam smirked at her when she made a face at his sarcasm. "I'm just trying to be helpful."

"Yeah, well…you're not."

He chuckled. "Why? Because I'm stating the obvious?"

Unfortunately, yes, she thought. And rather than examining that too closely, she decided to turn the tables on him. "So where did you and Mason go the other night? Anywhere fun?"

He shrugged. "You know, around. We hit up a few bars

and then...I drove him home. God forbid we stay out too late and upset Aunt Georgia."

It almost sounded plausible, except...he wouldn't look at her. Considering they were twins, she knew that was their tell–the one way to know when one of them wasn't being completely honest.

"And you just drove around and...what...had a couple of drinks? You didn't meet up with anyone? Pick up anyone at any of the places? That doesn't sound like you. I can't speak for Mason..."

Another shrug. "Nah, it wasn't like that. We just hung out and...you know...talked. I don't have to hook up with someone every time I go out."

Mallory slammed her hand down hard on the desk, causing Sam to jump. "Oh, my gosh! Stop lying!"

"What the hell are you talking about? I'm not!"

"You so are!" Shaking a finger at him, she stood up and leaned over the desk toward him. "For starters? You and Mason never hang out and talk. Next, any time you go anywhere in this town, you always hit on some random girl and try to hook up. So the fact that you're sitting here telling me you didn't, and all you did was talk to Mason absolutely screams of you being a big fat liar!"

"Hey!" He jumped to his feet.

"Why are you being so evasive? What could you have possibly done this time?"

His head lolled back and he growled before looking at her again. "Okay, fine," he snapped. Turning, he shut the office doors and then leaned against them when he faced her. "We really did just go to hang out. Like I said the other night, Mason is way more tolerable now. He said he was stressed and just needed to get out and it didn't seem like a bad idea. We grabbed a six-pack and went down to the beach to just chill."

"So what happened?"

He shrugged again. "We drank and we talked. He's freaking miserable. Aunt Georgia and Uncle Beau really dictate everything he does and as much as he's tried to play along all these years, he's kind of hit his limit."

"Wow..."

"I know. So he was talking about wanting to move away, start a new career...it was crazy. Next thing I know we're out of beer and we go and buy another six-pack."

"Oh, no..."

He nodded. "I know. That's when I should have realized we were in trouble."

"Did you get pulled over?"

He let out a mirthless laugh. "Not exactly."

"What does that even mean?" Honestly, it was beginning to feel like she was never going to know what happened. "Sam?"

"We went to go back to the beach, but there was a patrol car in the parking lot. So we drove down Main Street and decided to just pull into the church parking lot to finish drinking and talking."

"Ew...you drank beer in the church parking lot? What is wrong with you? That's just wrong."

"Yeah, well...we thought it would be fine and no one would bother us. But..." He sighed. "After all those beers we were both feeling a little stupid and weren't thinking clearly. I had to pee so..."

Suddenly it hit her. "You didn't."

But he nodded. "I did."

"Sam..." she whined.

"Actually, we both did. And we were laughing hysterically and didn't realize how loud we were and...next thing you know, Pastor Steve is out there chasing us around threatening to call the cops!" Then he laughed. "We were both running around with our dicks hanging out and jumped into the car and sped away!"

"No!"

But he nodded again. "I still can't believe anyone was there! I mean, who would have thought the pastor would be hanging out at the church at that hour of night!"

She groaned. "That's completely not the point. You guys are gross."

He laughed lowly. "I swear, I don't know how I got Mason home without killing both of us and then getting back here. I keep waiting for the cops to show up or–at the very least–Pastor Steve to show up here along with Aunt Georgia! So I'm kind of lying low."

"If you're trying to lie low, where were you just before?"

"Working in the yard. The tree company cleared away all the debris but what's left back there is still a mess. I wanted to clean the flower beds and see what could be salvaged and what needed to be replaced. We were able to get some fresh mulch out of it all though." Another shrug. "I know that's what Pops would have done."

As much as Mallory wanted to be mad at her brother for being such a moron, he went and somewhat redeemed himself by doing something selfless. Unable to help herself, she walked around the desk and hugged him.

"You're an idiot. You know that, right?"

He hugged her back. "I know. But I swear I've learned my lesson."

"I hope so. The last thing anyone needs right now is you on the front page of the local newspaper because you peed on a church."

"It wasn't on the church, just...on church property."

With a playful punch, she stepped back. "Don't split hairs with me on this. You were still wrong." She gave him a sad smile. "Seriously, we are both a mess."

And in a very un-Sam-like move, he pulled her back in for another hug. "Yeah, but my money's on you, kiddo. You're going to be just fine. I know it."

She only wished she had his confidence.

On Monday morning, Jake was over at Zeke's place as the crew was getting started on the re-framing of the addition and building a new deck. It was early and he'd slept alone the night before, so he was anxious to see Mallory.

"Hey, there you are," he said with a smile as he walked into the kitchen carrying a box from her favorite bakery.

She smiled at him and then caught a glimpse of the pink box. "Hey," she said as she sauntered over. "What's in the box?"

With a careless shrug, he leaned in and kissed her on the cheek. "Maybe some chocolate croissants." He paused. "Maybe a couple of jelly donuts. You know, no big deal."

"Jake Summerford do not tease me about baked goods," she exclaimed, but Jake was having too much fun.

"And I think...I think there might be either a chocolate chip muffin or some sort of crumb cake." He shrugged. "I don't know. I just told Mrs. Henderson – whose hair is currently the shade of cotton candy - to throw any old thing in the box that nobody else would want."

Laughing, she playfully punched him in the arm and took the box from his hands. Once she placed it on the table, she turned and kissed him–her arms wrapping around him slowly enough to make him want to haul her in close. It wasn't a quick kiss either. No, his girl put a lot of effort into thanking him and now he wished he knew for certain that they were alone because he could think of a few ways he'd love to start the day.

"Oh, good morning, Jake! You're here early!" Susannah said cheerily. "Oh, you went to Henderson's this morning?"

The sound Mallory made in his ear was part chuckle part whine and he knew her mind was drifting in the same direction as his. He placed a light kiss on her cheek before turning her toward the table and urging her to sit. "Ladies," he said with a big smile, "enjoy."

When he went to leave the kitchen, Mallory stood and walked back over to him. "You're leaving already?"

Reaching out, he caressed her cheek and smiled warmly at her. "Just wanted to bring you breakfast since you weren't at my place this morning for me to make it for you."

She blushed and she was beautiful.

Combing her dark hair behind her ear, Jake leaned in close and kissed her again. She was wearing a pair of yoga pants, an oversized t-shirt, and didn't have on a stitch of makeup and she was still the most beautiful girl he had ever seen.

Not a girl, a woman, he reminded himself. Mallory Westbrook was no longer a girl and the woman she was now was the woman he wanted forever.

He just had to prove that to her.

"I need to go out and make sure the crew is getting started both in the front and back." He looked over at Susannah. "It's going to be pretty noisy here for the next week or so, so if you have things to do during the day to avoid it, I'd suggest you do that. Sorry."

"Don't apologize, Jake," Susannah replied, pouring

herself a cup of coffee. "I'd rather get this stuff banged out at the same time rather than drag it out for weeks. Thanks for getting everyone here so fast. I know there are a lot of places in greater need of repairs than here, but..."

He held up a hand to stop her. "I'm just doing what Zeke would have wanted, that's all." He gave Mallory a gentle nudge toward the kitchen table again. "Go eat," he said before looking at Susannah again. "Have you given any more thought about what you might want to work on here in the house next?"

She looked nervously at Mallory before looking back at him. "Um..." then she nodded toward the doorway and he took that as his hint that she wanted to talk to him alone.

Weird...

One last glance at Mallory showed she was equally perplexed by her mother's response, but she stayed at the table and waved goodbye to him. Susannah didn't stop walking until they were in Zeke's office where she shut the door behind them.

Okay, super weird...

"Jake," she began, her voice little more than a whisper, "I need to ask you something." She sat down behind the massive desk and Jake took a seat in front of it.

"What's going on, Susannah?"

She let out a long breath before looking at him again. "Okay, here's the thing–you spent a lot of time with my grandfather and...you seem like you know a lot more about what he wanted done with this house than any of us."

"I wouldn't say that..."

"Please," she interrupted with a small smile. "We both know you do and it's really okay. I...I was curious if he mentioned to you what it was that I had mentioned wanting to do with the house...in the future."

It took a minute for Jake to realize what she was getting at and nodded. "You mean how you want to turn the place into a bed and breakfast."

Sagging with relief, Susannah nodded. "Yes. It was something he and I started talking about in the last several months and I wasn't sure if he was paying attention or if it was something he was okay with." She paused. "You know how he was–he was a great listener but there were times when he wasn't very clear with his feelings."

"Oh, I don't know about that. I seem to remember Zeke being very vocal when he was opposed to something. If he didn't shut you down while you were talking to him about it, I would guess he wasn't completely against the idea."

"Did he ever mention it to you?"

"Just in passing and I thought it was just him rambling on about what he thought would happen once he was gone. Every once in a while he'd do that sort of thing. He'd talk about what he thought would happen once he wasn't around to make sure everyone was okay."

"So...what do you think? Is this something I should be considering if we move forward with renovations on the house?"

"That's completely up to you, Susannah. I don't want to weigh in on this because...well..."

"Oh, please," she said again. "My grandfather was closer to you than anyone–and that's saying something because he was extremely close to Mallory." Then she paused and considered him. "You know that's one of the things that made him happiest, don't you?"

He shook his head, unsure of what she was saying.

"When you and Mallory first started dating, Pops wasn't so thrilled. He didn't like thinking that Mallory wasn't a little girl anymore. But as the summer wore on, he came to really like the idea of the two of you together. I think he was just as upset as the two of you when you broke up."

"Yeah, we had talked about it after Mallory left. Zeke was pretty adamant about me going to college and not letting Mallory be a deciding factor. That was part of the conversation she overheard but didn't understand," he explained. "He knew how much getting an education meant to me and knew if I could do that–if I could move so far away from my family and everything I had ever known and make that dream possible–then I could do anything." He paused with a lopsided grin. "Including taking care of his great-granddaughter."

Susannah leaned back in the big leather chair and smiled. "I swore I wouldn't pry and I swear this isn't why I brought you in here..."

"I know." He grinned. "And I want you to know your daughter means everything to me. But I broke her trust once before and I have to work a bit harder this time around to win it back."

"She can be stubborn..."

Jake laughed out loud at that one. "That she is!"

"Right now...she's very emotional. Losing Pops hit her so much harder than I ever imagined. So maybe the timing for the two of you...maybe you could give her some time."

"I will, Susannah. I promise you. I don't want to add any pressure to her and I don't want her making a decision she'll come to regret."

"But...?"

He chuckled softly. "But I need to do this my way this time. I feel like that summer had a lot of pressure from all kinds of other people and our time wasn't really our own."

"What can I do?"

"That's just it. I don't want you or Sam or her cousins to do anything. Right now, if everyone starts talking to her about moving here or badgering her about our relationship, it will make her skittish–which she already is."

Susannah nodded.

"Just know, I have big hopes for our future."

And that seemed to please her immensely. "Okay, then." She paused and shifted in her chair again. "Now about this bed and breakfast idea..."

———

It was lunchtime before Jake had time to even breathe. There were easily twenty crewmen here at the house and with two separate projects going on at the same time, things were mildly chaotic. All the permits were in place, the property was clear, but it just seemed as if everyone and their brother had questions for him. On top of that, he had four other job sites up and running all over town that were calling in with updates as well. All he wanted was an hour to himself and something to eat.

As if reading his mind, Mallory came out onto the front porch with a large cooler bag in her hand and a sweet smile on her face. She practically skipped down the steps toward where he was standing talking to his foreman, Colton.

"Hey! What's in the bag?" he asked.

Looking at Colton, she said, "Do you mind if I borrow the boss for a lunch break?"

Colton, who had been with Coleman's almost as long as Jake had been alive, smiled and nodded. "See you in an hour, boss." And then he was gone.

Mallory took Jake's hand in hers and led him around the side of the house. "Where are we going?"

"You'll see," she said, grinning at him over her shoulder.

Two minutes later they were walking down the pier toward the boathouse. Mallory opened the door and stepped inside. The small air conditioning unit was on and the bistro table was set for two. It pleased him more than he could say that she had gone through the trouble to do this for him. If they had gone to eat in the main house, he would have been distracted by the work being done. This was the perfect reprieve from the noisy construction zone.

"I made us some chicken salad sandwiches and a fruit salad," she said as she put the food on the table. "There are cold drinks in the mini-fridge over there so help yourself, and for dessert, I baked cookies."

"A girl after my own heart," he said, grabbing her and kissing her soundly. And as good as the menu sounded, he wouldn't mind putting the food on hold so he could have her for lunch–an idea he ran by her before he let her go.

"A nooner, huh? Hmm...let me think about that."

The next thing Jake knew, Mallory was standing beside him and unzipping her sundress that began to pool at her feet.

He loved when she wore dresses for this exact reason.

She struck a sassy pose with her hands on her hips and she was a sweet, innocent, and sexy siren all at the same time. "So you're saying...we should put lunch on hold so we can...hmm...what would you call it?"

He was already kicking his shoes off and pulling his shirt over his head. "I'd call it time for me to devour you for making me sleep alone last night."

After that, the only sound was Mallory's squeal of delight as he picked her up and dropped her on the sofa. She had barely settled against the cushions when Jake was sprawled out on top of her, loving the feel of her curves under him.

"If I promise that you won't have to sleep alone tonight, does that mean we can't do this again tomorrow?"

Smiling against her throat, Jake gently bit her. "You already planning on doing this again tomorrow?"

Arching her back beneath him, she all but moaned his name. "I've got the entire week planned out if you must know."

And just that one simple reminder of how all they had was this week was enough to make him pause. One week. He had one week to convince her to stay and give them a chance. One week to prove to her that he's not the same man he was six years ago.

One week to convince her to fall in love with him again.

Because he sure as hell was still in love with her.

Yeah, part of him had always known it, but he thought he'd get over it—particularly after the cold shoulder she gave him for years. But once they got past that, he knew his feelings weren't going to change. Mallory Westbrook was it for him.

She whispered his name as her nails raked their way down his back and it brought him out of his reverie.

"The whole week, huh?"

She nodded.

"You may need to pack a bigger lunch, because I plan on us using every ounce of energy we have. Every. Single. Day."

Then he immediately went to work on doing just that on day one.

8

"*WHAT?!*"

All heads turned as Georgia Coleman-Bishop shrieked at the attorney in a very un-Southern belle-like way. Mallory had to stifle a giggle and beside her, she saw her brother fighting to hold on to his own composure. Even though no one had any idea what Pops had put in his will, she didn't think anyone could have predicted this kind of reaction to anything.

Richard McClellan was an older gentleman–easily in his mid-sixties–and was the family attorney for as long as Mallory could remember. His expression at Georgia's outburst was almost as comical as the outburst itself.

"There has got to be some mistake," Aunt Georgia demanded as she stood and fanned herself, towering over Richard's desk. "This has to be either an old will or my grandfather wasn't in his right mind when he wrote it!" She looked over her shoulder at Mallory's mother and fumed. "You! You convinced him to do this, didn't you? That's why you came back here! To take my inheritance away from me!"

"Georgia," Susannah began calmly, but Mallory knew her mother was holding on to her patience by a thread. "When has anyone ever convinced Pops to do anything he didn't want to do? Now stop this nonsense and sit down!"

"I will not..."

Just then, Beau stood up and guided his wife back to her seat and warned her "That's enough" before sitting beside her.

Clearing his throat, Richard looked nervously at the room full of people. They had originally planned to have him come to the house to read the will, but with all the construction going on, it was decided they'd all come to his office. Luckily it was a room large enough to house the fifteen people Pops had named in his will.

"Okay, if I may continue?" he asked the group as a whole, and everyone nodded. "The house goes to my granddaughter, Susannah Coleman-Westbrook, to turn into the bed and breakfast she has always wanted to own. There is an account already set aside with money for you to do the renovations." He paused and smiled at her. "I have an envelope with the account information for you, Susannah," he explained before handing her the envelope.

"Thank you," she whispered as she accepted it.

Looking back down at the papers in his hands, Richard continued. "To my granddaughter, Georgia Coleman-Bishop, and her husband Beau Bishop, I leave my boat and the Magnolia Marina. As you know, I built that as a young man and I know Beau has always enjoyed sailing and Georgia has enjoyed the benefits of the marina's club." He paused and–like everyone else in the room–looked over at Georgia to see her reaction.

She gave a curt nod of approval but still managed a quick glare at Susannah.

This is going to be interesting, Mallory thought. There was no doubt this was going to cause a rift in the family for a long time to come.

After another moment, Richard went on. "I am certain that my grandson Cash did not show for the reading of my will. There is a trust set up for him, but he must be present here in Magnolia Sound in order to receive it. However, to his wife Grace–who is far too forgiving–I leave you the money to pay for college for all three boys, plus the mortgage on your home will be paid in full."

Grace openly wept and Mallory knew she–just like everyone else in the room–knew how much Pops had done with those two simple gifts. He was giving her aunt the breathing room she so desperately needed. Her uncle had been gone for years–hell, Mallory barely remembered him. He'd left his wife and sons because he wanted something more out of life. Her poor aunt was left to raise three young boys and her uncle only sporadically checked in to make sure they were okay. What kind of person did that?

"Now, in the order of their births, I would like to address my great-grandchildren," Richard read, and Mallory forced herself to focus.

"Sam and Mallory," he began, looking at her and Sam. "When the two of you were born, I couldn't have been prouder. With you living so far away, I never thought I'd get to be involved in your lives. Twins didn't run in our family and whenever I got to see the two of you, you were both an oddity and a complete joy to me."

Susannah took Mallory's hand in hers and smiled before leaning forward to smile at Sam too.

"There are some personal letters I've written to the two of you that Richard will give you after we get through everything," Richard read, "but I want you both to know I always treasured our time together." He paused. "To my great-grandson Sam, I leave you Coleman Landscaping. You're the only one in this family with a green thumb and I hope you choose to run the company yourself."

Richard then looked over at Mallory and her heart began to beat like mad. What would Pops possibly leave her? She'd give anything to have him here with her instead of some inheritance.

"Mallory, I know you pride yourself on being some sort of fancy technology girl and I'm so proud of all you've accomplished even though I never understood any of it. But I remember watching the joy on your face when you paint and how happy you always looked when you were decorating or being creative. I never want you to lose that joy. I'm leaving you something I don't think you were even aware I owned–Barb's Beach Buys."

Gasping, Mallory squeezed her mother's hand. She really had no idea Pops owned the place and it was her favorite store in all of Magnolia Sound. She hadn't been there since last summer and had heard Barb wanted to retire. Could Pops have known that back then and planned for her to take over all this time?

"On top of that," Richard continued, "Mallory is in charge of the decorating and renovating of the house, along-side Susannah. I want the two of them to do this together and make the bed and breakfast a place that honors everything Magnolia Sound represents."

Everything became a blur after that. Mallory couldn't focus on what Richard was reading and what Pops had left to her cousins. Her mind was reeling, and all she wanted to do was step outside and get some air. She looked over her shoulder and saw Jake sitting behind her smiling. God...she wanted to talk to him too. So many questions and so many things to consider and she had no idea what she was going to do about any of it.

Clearly the business was still up and running and could continue to do so even if she didn't live here. If Barb retired, there would still be a staff employed who could run the place in Mallory's absence. It wasn't necessarily a necessity for her to move here to run the shop. Plus, could she really make a living from owning the shop, doing decorating consultations and nothing else?

That had her thinking about looking for a business advisor—someone who could look over the finances for the business so Mallory could make informed decisions. Did she know anyone who did that? Maybe her mother did? Or maybe her cousins? Maybe she should talk to Richard about it.

Her head was starting to hurt just trying to organize her thoughts. When she turned to look at her brother, she saw he looked equally dazed. No doubt taking over a local landscaping business wasn't on his agenda either—especially since he went to business school and currently had a job doing...wait, what was Sam doing these days? He did tend to change jobs a lot and seemed to get bored easily. Was it a bank he was at now or a doctor's office where he was doing data entry? She shook her head because she couldn't remember and it was too much to think of on top of all her own stuff.

Doing her best to clear her head, Mallory turned her attention back to Richard and whoever he was addressing next.

"And lastly, Jake Summerford."

She wanted to turn around so badly and watch him and silently cursed herself for not sitting with him. He had arrived a little late and by the time he walked in,

Mallory was already situated between her mother and brother.

Casually, she slid her hand back between her and Sam's chair and hoped Jake would see it. His hand immediately clasped hers and she knew he was just as nervous as she'd been a few minutes ago.

"Jake, you've always been like family to me and watching you learn the construction business always made me feel proud. I can't think of anyone I'd trust more than you to take the business over and make it grow. Coleman Construction is yours."

It was hard to hold in the gasp as Jake squeezed her hand ridiculously hard. Turning, she looked at him and smiled. She saw tears in his eyes and wanted to climb over the chairs to comfort him. Luckily, Richard was wrapping things up and within minutes, she was out of her seat and in Jake's arms.

"I never..." he began, his voice soft and trembling. "I never thought he'd do something like that. I knew someone was going to take over and...and I thought he'd have someone lined up to buy the company. So many times I wanted to ask him about buying it because...well...I just always knew it was where I wanted to work. And to know it's mine?" He stopped talking and buried his face in her neck and Mallory felt his tears. She held him tightly for several long moments and when they broke apart, she saw he looked a little more composed.

"You okay?" she asked.

Nodding, he gave her a soft kiss. "Sorry about that. I just...he did so much for me already that I never expected anything like this. It's more than I deserve."

"No, it's not. You have been the one handling things for so long, I think you were the natural choice. Pops believed in you," she said. Her voice caught and she took a minute to compose herself before she began to cry. "Now you need to believe in yourself."

After that it seemed like everyone wanted to talk. Richard walked around and answered questions even as he handed out envelopes that held letters Pops wrote to everyone. Mallory had to hand it to him—he knew how to make an impact on his family even after he was gone.

"Oh, my gosh," Parker said as she walked over with a big smile on her face. "Can you believe all of this? I mean...who knew Pops paid attention to so much!"

"What are you talking about?"

"Come on—leaving you the decorating place? That was awesome! And Jake and the construction company? Perfect!"

"I hate to say this, but...I sort of zoned out there for a while. What did Pops leave you?"

"That's the beautiful thing—he didn't leave me a business or anything here in Magnolia!" she explained excitedly.

"And...you're okay with that?"

She nodded enthusiastically. "Oh, God yes! I know my parents want me to stay here and follow in their footsteps and all that crap, but I want to make my own decisions and I want to travel and now I can!"

"So...Pops left you....?"

"A trust fund that I get next year!" She told Mallory the amount he left in trust and she had to admit, she was impressed. For a man who had so much money, it was odd that he never flaunted it or even talked about it.

"That's amazing, Parks. Really. I'm sure you already have a list of places you want to go and things you want to do, huh?"

"You know it!"

"Ugh...is she gloating over here?" Peyton asked as she walked over and joined them. "Because I have a feeling baby girl is gloating."

"May-be," Parker said with a big grin before smacking her older sister's arm. "And what are you complaining about? You got Cafe Magnolia! You love that place!"

It's true, Peyton loved cooking and had hoped to go to culinary school, but her parents encouraged her to get a "real degree," as they called it. Looks like the business degree they forced on her could come in handy when running her own business.

"That is so cool, Peyton! Your own restaurant! Aren't you excited?" Mallory asked.

Peyton shrugged. She was a couple of years younger than Mallory and nowhere near as studious or mature. If anything, she was the typical middle child who had done her share of acting out to get attention. Maybe having the responsibility of her own restaurant was a little daunting to her right now.

"I know Dennis is getting ready to retire," Peyton said quietly, "and the timing is right for someone to come in and take over, but...I didn't expect it to be me! I'm not ready for it."

"I heard Dennis already found his replacement," Parker said casually. "You're going to have to go in there and start talking to everyone fast before it gets too chaotic. Too many changes at one time can't be good for business, right?"

If Peyton felt half as overwhelmed as Mallory did, she was sure this conversation wasn't helping. "What about Gertie?" she asked, changing the subject. "Like I said, I zoned out and missed most of the reading. When I looked for her after everything was done, she was wiping away tears as her granddaughter walked out with her."

"It was nice of Mary Jane to come with her," Peyton said. "You know Gertie can't drive herself around much these days."

Mallory wasn't aware of that so she simply nodded.

"Remember how she always used to say she was going to retire in St. Thomas because that's where her grandparents were from?"

She nodded.

"Well, Pops bought her a place there and left her enough money to make the move and retire," Parker said with a sad smile. "It will feel so weird not to have Gertie around. Her cooking is legendary in this family."

Peyton cleared her throat. "Um...I'm a good cook too, you know."

"Not like Gertie," Parker murmured.

Sadly, Parker was right. Gertie had been cooking for them their entire lives and just the thought of not enjoying any more of her meals or sitting around the kitchen talking to her just added a whole other level of sadness to the whole situation. She sighed.

"And did you hear what Mason got?" Parker whispered with a bit of a snarky grin.

Mallory shook her head.

"Oh, my gosh, his face was priceless!" Peyton said with a grin of her own. "I can't even begin to imagine what Pops was thinking!"

"Mal?" Sam called out, interrupting the conversation. "C'mon, we're going back to the house."

"Okay, give me a minute," she replied and was surprised when he stalked across the room and glared at Parker and

Peyton before looking at her again. "Now. Mom's upset and we need to go."

Saying a quick goodbye to the girls, Mallory turned and walked out of the room with Jake right behind her. They were outside walking across the parking lot when he stopped her. "Maybe we should just plan on seeing each other later."

"What? No, why?"

"Your mom's upset and I'm pretty sure your aunt is the reason. I doubt she wants me hanging around to witness it all."

He had a point, but...

"I still want you there and besides, you'll be a good distraction when we get her to start thinking about all the changes she wants to make to the house. I have a feeling we're going to have to get her to focus on that instead of how angry she is with Aunt Georgia."

"Are you sure?"

Leaning in, she kissed him.

"Mallory!" Sam called out from beside their mother's car.

"I'm riding home with Jake!" And for some reason, it felt really good to say that out loud.

Growing up, Jake's parents had argued in front of him and had no problem venting when they were frustrated with whatever was going on in their lives. Sitting back and watching the Westbrooks handle the situation with their inheritances, though, was like nothing he had ever seen.

"Who does she think she is—accusing me of strong-arming Pops into leaving me this house?" Susannah cried as soon as they were in the door. "No one ever told that man what to do and she knows it! Maybe she should consider the fact that he knew she was just being a gold-digger and didn't want to leave it to her!" She tossed her purse on the living room sofa and began to pace. "Did you know she wanted to put Pops in a home last year? And she wasn't even shy about making plans for this place right in front of him!"

Jake remembered that whole shit-show. Zeke was livid and vowed that Georgia would never get her hands on his house.

And clearly, Ezekiel Coleman was a man of his word.

"She already has so damn much!" Susannah was saying. "Beau is beyond wealthy and they have more than anyone I know and yet she still wants more! And she doesn't want anyone else to have anything either! Everything should go to her or her kids and..." She groaned. "She's impossible!"

No one disagreed.

"What am I supposed to do, huh? How am I supposed to just...go ahead with my plans for the house with her being so unreasonable?"

Jake looked at Sam and Mallory and saw that neither seemed to know what to say.

But he did.

"Excuse me for saying so, Susannah, but...what difference does it make what Georgia thinks? The house is yours. Your name is going on the deed, the account for the renovation will be in your name...the way I see it, Georgia can't stop you."

"What if she contests the will?"

Jake grinned. "I guess you missed Richard's disclaimer at the beginning of the reading."

All three Westbrooks looked at him.

"Anyone who contests the will, loses their inheritance

as will their children," he said with a grin. "You don't think for a second that Zeke didn't know Georgia was going to freak out when she found out you got the house, do you?"

"I don't remember him saying that," Susannah said, slowly sitting down on the sofa. "I guess there was so much legalese that I missed it."

"I remember him saying it," Sam said frowning. "So now I'm stuck with a business I don't want."

"What? How could you not want it?" his mother asked. "It's the perfect job for you! You love working in the yard!"

"Not as a career, Mom!" he countered. "I'm going to sell the business. It's the only solution."

"Um..." Jake began hesitantly. "Have you guys looked at your letters from Zeke yet?"

They all shook their heads.

"Maybe you should before you make any rash decisions," he said and hated how he had been privy to so many of Zeke's thoughts before he died. Granted, he had no idea what any of them were getting—except for Sam—but he wasn't about to share that information.

Out of all his grandchildren and great-grandchildren, Sam was the one Zeke worried about the most. He knew Sam was a hell-raiser who was constantly in trouble, and most of the time he attributed it to the fact that Susannah's husband had left and there hadn't been a positive male role model in Sam's life on a full-time basis. Over the years, Zeke had talked about wanting Sam to grow up and settle down—not so much with a wife and kids, but just...calming down on his wild and impetuous ways.

About a year ago, Sam got arrested. The only reason Jake knew about it was because he had been here when Susannah got the call. It was for a DUI and Sam spent a night in jail, but Zeke had demanded he come here and talk to him in person. Sam had and Zeke laid down the law for him–either get his shit together, or he was going to be disowned. It seemed drastic, but Sam had taken the warning seriously and for the last year it seemed like he was doing okay. Looking at his face now, however, Jake saw traces of the angry and defiant man who had shown up here a year ago.

Not a good sign.

In the letter Zeke wrote, there was most likely a demand that Sam work the company for a year. It was something they had talked about because Zeke knew Sam would reject the idea of coming to work and live in Magnolia. He thought it would be good for Sam to have some family nearby and some stability in employment. If he opted not to stay for the year, the business would go to Mason and Sam would get no monetary gain from it.

He'd begged Zeke not to do it, and he honestly had no way of knowing for sure if he did until Sam read the letter.

And was it wrong that he secretly hoped there was a similar stipulation with Mallory's inheritance?

If she was forced to move back here for a year, he'd have more time to convince her that what they had was meant to be. But he also didn't want to be her fallback–a way to pass the time until she could leave. Even though that's what he originally went into this new phase of their relationship thinking, he now knew it was crazy. They weren't having a fling. This was the real deal.

He just needed Mallory to see it too.

They were all quiet for so long that he thought he'd go mad, but finally Susannah spoke up. "Jake, do you think...I mean...is it wrong that I want to do this? To turn this house into something new?"

He shook his head. "If anything, I think the timing is kind of perfect."

"What do you mean?" Mallory asked, sitting up a little straighter where she was on the sofa.

"The hurricane did so much damage to the town. What was once a neat and picturesque little town is now in shambles. We're going to be picking up the pieces for a long time. And, judging by Zeke's will, there's going to be a lot of new owners and management throughout the local businesses. I'd say Magnolia Sound is going through a bit of a transformation and wouldn't it be great to open the tourist season next summer with a new bed and breakfast?" he asked with a smile. "Think about all the marketing and promoting you could do for it. We always have a very active summer season and to have a place like this–a place with such a long-standing history within the town–would be a big draw. And depending on how big you want to go with this renovation, you could appeal to some very upscale clients."

He saw the smile on Susannah's face grow.

"And with Mallory helping with the design and decorating, you know it's going to be classy and elegant here." Then he looked at Sam. "And you are going to restore the grounds to the way your great-grandfather always had them–only better." He straightened and watched as their faces all seemed to transform from wariness to wonder. "What better testimony to the founding family of this town than restoring this place and preserving its history?"

Then, feeling a little smug, Jake walked over and sat down in one of the massive leather wingback chairs and smiled. "But that's just one way you can look at it."

And then everyone started talking at once.

"The addition could be turned into an apartment for me..."

"We need to think about adding another bathroom or two..."

"The nursery here in town doesn't offer enough inventory for me to do what needs to be done with the yard. Although I guess I could talk with them about special ordering stuff for me..."

"The wallpaper needs to be the first thing to go..."

"What about putting in commercial-grade appliances in the kitchen?"

Jake had a feeling this conversation was going to go on for a while and he opted to stand and excuse himself. Susannah and Sam both waved to him, but Mallory came over and kissed him goodbye and promised to see him later. And as he walked out of the house and looked at the construction equipment strewn all over the property, the enormity of what had been given to him today hit hard.

Walking quickly, he made his way back to his house and had his phone in his hand as soon as he walked through the door. He needed to talk to someone, and his father always had a way of helping him through some of life's harder moments.

"Jake! What a surprise! I figured you'd be busy for at least the next month or so before you'd have time to talk mid-day!" his father said with a small laugh. "Everything okay?"

God, where did he even begin?

Walking into the living room, he sat down on the sofa and let out a long breath. "We met with Zeke's attorney today for the reading of his will."

"Oh, Son, I'm sorry. I'm sure that was hard. How's everyone holding up? How's Mallory?"

Jake couldn't help but smile at the sound of her name. "She's hanging in there. Honestly, it's been hard on all of us.

Between the storm and Zeke dying, it feels like the entire world is upside down."

"Well, in some respects, it is." Jonah Summerford was almost always the voice of reason. He had a way of speaking plainly that Jake always appreciated. "Zeke has been a constant in Magnolia Sound for almost a century. He's been the one holding his family together for most of that time." He paused. "You know, it was so sad when we watched as he buried his wife and then his own children, but through it all, he was a rock for everyone. I imagine it's going to be a big adjustment for Susannah, Georgia, and all the great-grandkids."

"You have no idea..."

"What happened?"

Jake told him about the contents of the will and the argument between Susannah and Georgia and wasn't surprised when his father laughed.

"If you ask me, that's exactly as it should be. Georgia doesn't deserve the house. Susannah may have been gone for a long time, but she was always good to Zeke and I know he adored her–just like he does Sam and Mallory."

Then Jake told him about their inheritance.

"You know what, that makes total sense. Good for them!"

"I think Mallory's excited at the prospect, but Sam's not particularly thrilled."

"Sounds about right," Jonah responded thoughtfully. "Sam has never wanted to do what anyone tells him to do. No doubt he's fighting this simply because he's seeing it as Zeke telling him what to do one last time. I think in time he'll settle into it."

"I don't think Zeke gave him a choice." He explained the stipulations and his father laughed heartily and Jake couldn't help but join him. "I'll tell you something, Dad, Zeke was always crafty, but this whole will really proved it."

"Any other surprises?"

And that's when he told him about his own inheritance.

"Jake! That is incredible! You've always wanted to be the one running Coleman Construction and Zeke knew it too. Congratulations!"

Yeah, it had been something they had all talked about ever since Jake was eighteen. He just never thought it would happen quite like this.

"It's a big responsibility, Dad. We're super busy right now and there's so much going on and...I don't know...I'm a little overwhelmed."

"Nonsense. We both know you were already running the business. Nothing is going to change except a new title."

"Dad, you're over-simplifying. Of course things are going to change," he countered.

"I disagree. Your staff is still in place, Jake. Zeke wasn't running the day-to-day operations and you've been the one signing the paychecks for the last year ever since Darrel Johnson retired. So why do you think anything's going to change?"

"Because Zeke's not here for me to go to for advice on things related to the business," he said quietly. Closing his eyes, he rested his head back against the cushions and fought the urge to cry even as the sting of tears was already there. "Everyone looked at Zeke as an old man who was out of touch with what was going on with his businesses, but it's not true. He was still as sharp as a tack. He loved talking about the jobs we were working on and offering advice on where to get materials or who was the right choice to be the foremen on different jobs. Without him here..."

"You'll still know what to do, Son. Zeke has been

training you and prepping you for this for ten years. You need to believe in yourself. Zeke did."

And damn if that didn't make him want to break down even more. "I don't want to let him down…"

"You couldn't. It's not possible. What does Mallory say about all of this?"

Jake paused for a moment and realized he hadn't told his father–or anyone for that matter–about the change in his and Mallory's relationship. "Why do you ask?" he asked suspiciously.

"You know I've always adored that girl," Jonah explained. "Things didn't end well for the two of you way back when, but I would imagine you've had to spend some time together since Zeke's passing. And I would also imagine you were both able to put the past aside during this time."

He nodded even though no one could see.

"I know how close Mallory was to Zeke, and I just thought she would have said something when you found out about inheriting the business."

"We haven't really talked about it. As far as I can tell, no one's upset with it, but they were all a little distracted by the whole Georgia and Susannah thing." He still couldn't believe there had almost been a catfight in the lawyer's office. "I don't think anyone else wanted the business, but knowing how greedy Georgia is, maybe once the dust settles, she'll realize she could have sold the business for a lot of money."

Jonah laughed. "Let's hope she doesn't."

He shrugged. "I still feel a little out of my element, Dad."

"It's only natural. Your mentor is gone and you're now taking on a position that was his for a very long time. You've got some pretty big shoes to fill, but if anyone can do it, it's you."

That one statement had Jake starting to relax. "Thanks, Dad."

"I'm proud of you, Jake. You're the most hard-working man I've ever known–next to Zeke. You've always said how much you admired him and what a smart businessman he was. And if he thought to leave his biggest business to you, then you need to trust that you can handle it."

"Maybe..."

"No maybes about it. You're going to do amazing things, Jake. Your degree in architectural design is going to help move Coleman's into a whole other division. You're going to grow in ways that Zeke never did. But more than that, you're going to put your own stamp on the business and make it your own."

That sounded like the dream he always had. It was crazy how now that he had it, he was second-guessing himself. Maybe it was just his grief getting in his way. Or maybe it was the uncertainty of his relationship with Mallory that made him feel like this. Maybe tonight was the night he needed to broach the subject with her. After all, the timing wasn't particularly ideal for wooing her–not with all this new business with...well...their new businesses and the loss of the man they both admired.

"Okay, now that we've covered how you're going to kick some major butt and be a huge success in the construction world, why don't you tell me how things are really going between you and Mallory?"

And unable to help himself, Jake laughed. "Well...how much time do you have?"

9

"I'M STAYING ANOTHER WEEK."

Jake lifted his head from the pillow and sleepily looked at her. "Um...what?"

Nodding, she explained. "I...I didn't feel right leaving so soon. Yesterday was like a bit of a bombshell - learning about Mom and the house, me with the store, and Sam with the business. My head is still spinning," she said with a small laugh, but noticed Jake wasn't smiling. If anything, his gaze was more awake and intense.

Clearing her throat, she went on. "I'm going to go to the shop today and meet with Barb to start looking over the books and talk transition with her. You know, see how long she can stay on, what kind of staff she has, and how much time she thinks I'll need to be here and how much I can delegate to the staff."

Still no response.

Letting out a long breath, she went on. "Plus, Mom and I were talking design and decorating ideas yesterday after you left and I feel like we have so much to think about and

I'd like to be here at this stage before construction goes any further. I already have so many ideas!"

She wasn't even sure he had blinked.

"And don't even get me started on Sam. I think he's going to need me the most. He's coming slightly unhinged at the thought of taking on the landscaping business. I know in time it's going to be a great thing for him, but right now he's not seeing it. In the letter Pops left, he basically gave Sam three months to get his life in Virginia in order before he had to officially come back to Magnolia to take over. I thought it was a great idea but he's still not fully on board with the whole thing. Hopefully if I can spend some time with him and get him to calm down and listen for a bit, he'll be okay."

Rolling onto her side, Mallory huffed with annoyance. "Okay, what? What is your problem?"

"I don't have a problem."

And she might have believed him if he hadn't said it through clenched teeth.

"Seriously? You're going to lie there and deny that something's wrong? Because clearly your face hasn't gotten the message."

With a careless shrug, Jake rolled onto his back, hands stacked behind his head on the pillow, and stared at the ceiling. "It's early. That's all."

Yeah, she still wasn't buying it.

After the family meeting yesterday, Jake went to help the construction crew who were working on the deck. Sometime in the mid-afternoon, he'd left the property and gone to check on numerous other sites going on around town. He'd worked late and when Mallory knocked on his door at eight last night with dinner for him, she knew he was exhausted. They spent a couple of hours relaxing and watching TV before going to bed.

And suddenly Jake wasn't so exhausted.

Normally she would smile at the memory of all the ways he had pleasured her, but right now she was too distracted by his mood to think anything good. Maybe he was just tired, like he said, but...she'd never known him to be angry about it. Glancing over at the bedside clock, she noted it wasn't *that* early. Could he be upset because she hadn't talked to him about her decision last night? She would have thought he'd be happy she was staying–after all, he was the one who first mentioned it to her.

"You know, I would have thought you'd be happy I was staying an extra week," she said with a huff, kicking the blankets off and determined to get up and leave. "Maybe it wasn't a sincere request. Maybe you were happy I was going–you probably thought you'd ask just because it was the thing to do, but secretly knew I wouldn't agree. Well...you're off the hook."

Her feet never even touched the floor. Jake's arm banded around her waist and hauled her back beside him. The initial instinct was to fight him–to kick him and shove him away if needed –but it seemed petty and childish. So she simply went limp and figured she'd hear him out and then get up and leave.

"First of all, everything you just said is ridiculous," he stated firmly and Mallory could see he was holding on to his temper. "If I didn't want you to stay, I wouldn't have asked you to." He sighed loudly.

"Then what's the problem?" she cried. "I'm staying!"

"For one extra week!" he yelled back. "And in all your little descriptions of why you're staying, I wasn't mentioned once! How do you think that makes me feel?"

"Jake..."

"Was I even a contributing factor at all or should I be thankful that you're fitting me into your busy schedule?"

"Hey!"

"Well what am I supposed to think, Mallory?" He jumped up from the bed and quickly pulled on the jeans he discarded the night before. "Just what the hell is it we're doing here?"

She looked up at him with wide eyes. "We're...I mean...we talked about this and..."

Slamming both hands on the bed hard enough to make her bounce, he shouted, "Forget about what we said on that first night! Have you not noticed that this isn't casual? How this isn't just us passing the time? I'm crazy about you, dammit! I asked you to stay here in Magnolia because I want you here! Not just for an extra week or for a damn summer, but all the time! Like forever!"

She gasped and felt like she was going to be sick. Yes, she had felt that things had changed and it was no longer about getting each other out of their systems, but she pushed that aside because she figured it was just wishful thinking on her part. Why should this time around be any different, right?

But...that wasn't what he was saying right now. If she heard him correctly–and she hoped she did–he was talking long term. Forever was long term, right?

"Jake, I..."

"I get that your life is upside down right now. Hell, your whole family is in crisis and you want to be there for them, but...I'm in crisis too, you know! Do you know what went through my head after I found Zeke?"

She shook her head.

"You," he said, though his voice was calmer. "I was thinking about you and how you were going to be devastated by the news. I wished I could have been the one to tell you in person. I hated the thought of you finding out over the phone. And then I laughed at myself because you hadn't spoken to me in years and figured I was probably the last person you'd want to see or hear any kind of news from."

She had the decency to look away because she was ashamed.

"You've never been far from my mind, Mal, not in all these years. I stayed away because...because it seemed like what you wanted." He hung his head. "Plus, I felt really guilty about the way things ended between us." Lifting his head, he gave her a tortured look. "All the things I said to you? They were in the heat of the moment. I never...I didn't mean any of it. I purposely pushed you away because...at the time, it seemed like the right thing to do. For both of us."

Now she knew she was staring and her jaw just might be on the floor. "Um...what?" She scooted across the bed and away from him and yeah, she definitely felt sick now.

It was clear he could see her distress and when Jake tried to reach for her, Mallory recoiled. Hanging his head once again, he said, "I'm so sorry. You have no idea how much I hate what I did to you. To us."

Climbing from the bed, Mallory immediately began to get dressed. "Oh, you're sorry? Now? Six damn years later? What the hell, Jake!"

Straightening on the opposite side of the bed, he held up his hand helplessly. "Do you not remember everything that was going on back then, Mallory?"

"Of course I do! How could I possibly forget?"

"No," he interrupted firmly. "No, you need to hear me

out, dammit!" Then he paused and took a moment to calm down. "Nothing about our relationship was easy for me. I struggled with guilt about dating my mentor's great-grand-daughter more than you'll ever know." Another pause. "I struggled with seeing you as a woman after only thinking of you as a young girl. I worried about what Zeke would think, I worried about what your brother would think, but most of all, I worried that I wasn't good enough for you."

She did not want to be swayed by the things he was telling her, but dammit, it was hard not to be. Everything he said made sense and seemed completely logical, but part of her still really wanted to be mad.

"Then I was faced with losing my financial aid," he went on. "I had waited so long for everything to work out for me with going to school and I kept putting it off and putting it off and just when I was ready to do it, it was pulled away from me. Zeke's offer to help me was not an easy one to accept."

"Why?" she asked and hated that she needed to know.

He shrugged. "I wanted to do it all on my own. I didn't want to need anyone's help. Call it pride, but...it was impor-tant to me. That's why it took so long for me to finally make it happen. Zeke had offered to help me for years." He let out a mirthless laugh. "Before I had even graduated high school he was offering to pay for college for me because he believed in me–believed in what I could do with myself and my future. I turned him down every time and when he offered again that summer...I was torn."

She didn't have to ask why.

She was the reason.

"The thing is, he knew. He knew I was struggling and it was the first time I was honestly considering taking him up on his offer." He paused and gave her a sad smile. "That's what you heard that day when you were leaving. He forced me to make a decision I couldn't make on my own–and it was hard and it was painful, but...I can't regret it, Mallory. Even if it meant the end of us, we both had things we needed to accomplish and we both needed to grow up."

She bristled at his words–hating the reference to the way he'd mocked her immaturity.

"I know you're upset..."

"You don't know the half of it," she said quietly as she finished dressing. "I may have been immature back then and I may have reacted rashly when I overheard your conversation, but the fact is...you didn't care about me enough to talk to me. Maybe things still would have ended, but at least I would have known the truth." She shook her head. "I don't know if I can trust you, Jake."

Now it was his eyes that went wide with disbelief. "Excuse me?"

"You made a decision for me–for us–that devastated me. You had six years to tell me the truth, and you didn't. Then I come back here and you tell me we just need to keep it casual–no promises, no commitments–and then you once again go and try to make decisions for me!"

And then something hit her.

"Oh my God...did you know Pops was going to leave me the shop?"

"What? No! Of course not!"

"I don't believe you. You seemed to know about what Pops was doing for Sam, so it only makes sense you would know about my inheritance too!" She shook her head and began to pace. "It all makes sense now!"

"What the hell are you talking about?" he yelled, coming around the bed toward her.

"This! Us! I foolishly thought we were just going

to...you know...have a fling! A little closure! But all along you knew what Pops was going to offer me and knew–like Sam–I wouldn't be so keen on moving back here because of you! So you just...you schmoozed your way back into my life and made me fall for you again so I'd stay and honor his wishes!"

He shook his head as if to clear it. "Do you even hear yourself?" he cried. "So now, not only am I guilty of...of...not being trustworthy, but now I'm such a puppet to your grandfather, that I'd purposely make you fall back in love with me so you'd run a stupid decorating shop here in town? Is that what you're saying? Do you hear how freaking ridiculous you sound?"

Okay, when he put it that way it did sound crazy, but...

"You know what, I don't care how crazy or ridiculous it sounds," she countered. "The fact is that I don't trust you. There's too much going on and now every time I look at you and think things are going well, I'm going to feel like there are some ulterior motives or...or...that what you say isn't what you mean."

"Mallory, the only time I ever lied to you..."

"Was when I was so damn in love with you and you broke my heart," she said sadly, willing the tears that were stinging her eyes not to fall. "If you had only talked to me..."

He reached for her, but she took a step back.

"We still would be where we are right now," he said, his voice low and gruff. "There was never going to be a scenario where things worked, Mal. I was always going to Colorado and you were always going back to New York. I know we said we'd try the long-distance thing, but...in the end it wouldn't have worked."

One lone tear rolled down her cheek and she silently

cursed it even as she wiped it away. "Here's the thing, Jake...we'll never know. Maybe it wouldn't have worked, but there wouldn't have been such hard feelings. I wouldn't have stayed away from coming here to visit Pops. I wouldn't have missed my last chance to..."

And dammit, now she was crying–was so blinded by tears that she couldn't have moved if she wanted to.

And unfortunately, she didn't see Jake stepping in close until his arms were around her.

She cried the way she had six years ago.

She cried the way she had two weeks ago when she learned about Pops.

But mostly, she cried like a woman whose entire world had been ripped apart without any hope of it being right ever again.

Especially since it seemed like no matter what happened, she was somehow forever going to be connected to Jake Summerford and Magnolia Sound whether she wanted to be or not.

And for the first time in her entire life, the thought of living here in this town was the very last thing she wanted.

She had walked through the doors of this shop dozens of times in her life, but this was the first time she was doing it as the owner.

She owned a business.

One of the many places in Magnolia Sound that she loved.

With a steadying breath, Mallory smoothed a hand over her hair and did her best to keep a serene smile on her face.

Even though the entire morning had been beyond traumatic for her.

Pushing the glass door open, she stepped into Barb's Beach Buys and let out a long breath. Hers, this place was hers. Slowly, she began to walk around the large showroom and touch and admire things. She was so lost in her own thoughts that she didn't notice Barb standing in the back corner watching her. When she finally did, Mallory felt herself blush with embarrassment.

Making her way toward her, she smiled. "Hey, Barb. It's nice to see you again."

She was expecting maybe a handshake or a more professional greeting, but instead, Barb Harper walked right up to her and pulled her into an exuberant embrace. "Mallory Westbrook, you have no idea how thrilled I am that this place is going to you!"

Taking a step back, Mallory studied her. "Really?"

Barb nodded. "You are going to be the perfect owner! I knew it the first time you came in here!"

That made Mallory chuckle softly. "I was twelve back then."

"But you had an eye for décor!" Barb cried. "I saw the appreciation you had for the pieces in here and the way you talked about how you would group items together. Oh, how I used to enjoy watching you!"

And her blush deepened. "Can I ask you something?"

"Of course!" Barb paused and looked around. "Why don't we sit down and get comfortable? I'm sure you have lots of questions about the place."

It was true, but there was one that she simply had to have the answer to first.

"How is it that Pops owned this place when it's your name on the sign?"

Now it was Barb's turn to blush. She fidgeted in the white rocking chair she chose to sit in before looking at Mallory. "About ten years ago, I thought I was going to have to close the shop."

"What? I don't remember that!"

Nodding, Barb said. "It's true. I fell down the stairs that winter. I really did a number on my back and broke my leg. I was running the place essentially on my own so when I couldn't work..."

"The store didn't open," Mallory finished for her.

"I was devastated. This place isn't much, but it was mine and I built it up from nothing," she said with a hint of fierceness. "As you can imagine in a town like this, everyone knew of my struggles. Zeke came to me and offered to buy the place but he'd let me keep running it. The only ones who knew of the arrangement were the two of us. Well, the two of us and my husband, Gary." She smiled. "I know this is going to sound weird, but...we're really excited that you're finally here to take over. I'm sorry it happened this way, but it gives me so much peace knowing my baby is in good hands."

As much as Mallory wanted to be pleased, it wasn't quite so cut-and-dried.

"Do you have a staff now or is it still just you? I thought I remember seeing some part-time helpers here..."

"I have a wonderful staff and we were all so relieved that our showroom was spared during the storm. We have a small warehouse full of inventory that suffered some water damage, but it's all covered by insurance so you'll be starting with a clean slate where that's concerned."

And that's when it hit her that there was so much she was going to have to deal with – inventory, learning the entire business, meeting vendors...it was a lot to take in. But as she looked around the room, she felt…invigorated. Was she nervous? Sure! This was all new to her. The thing that had her most excited was that this was a place that would always make her feel close to Pops. He had done this for her.

And maybe for Barb. Which reminded her…

"So what are your plans for retirement? Are you going to travel?"

"Not right away. I was figuring you might need me here for a while until you get settled. This all happened so suddenly and I'm sure you weren't planning on moving here tomorrow," she said with a sweet smile. Placing one hand over Mallory's, she gave it a light squeeze. "I won't walk away until you're ready. I want you to know that you're not alone. The girls and I are here to help."

Mallory let out a breath that she didn't realized she was holding. "I'm so glad! I was so nervous! This is all so new and…"

"It's a lot, I know. But like I said, you're not alone. There are three of us here – four or more during the summer months when we're busier – but if you're ever feeling overwhelmed, all you have to do is call."

For a minute, she was too overwhelmed to speak.

"Carol Taylor is my go-to girl here," Barb explained. "She's been with me almost ten years, ever since I was able to re-open the shop. Then there's Nicole Walters. She's young – a senior in high school – but she is a fantastic sales-girl. Blonde hair, blue eyes…she is completely adorable! And then we have Bree. She's a bit older than you and she's married with two little ones, so this job is a bit of a necessity and escape for her."

Laughing softly, Mallory said, "I can only imagine!"

"They are the best staff a girl could ask for. I believe I'll be leaving you in very capable hands."

Mallory had to agree. "How about we get started?"

Two days later, Jake still had no idea what went wrong.

For the life of him, he thought they were going in the right direction but when it came right down to it, they weren't on the same page on anything. And on top of that, Mallory was always going to blame him for her not coming home this summer.

And that was the one thing he knew he could never make up for.

Even if he spent every day of the rest of his life proving to her how much he loved her and wanted to be with her, he can't give her back the time she missed with Zeke.

"Jake!" Colton called out. They were working on Zeke's place–well, now Susannah's place–and he found some issues with the addition now that everything was down to the studs.

"What's going on?"

"Well, we found something and...um..."

He really didn't have the time or patience for this right now. "Just get to the point, Colt. We've got a lot going on here and I'm sure Susannah would like to have a little peace and quiet back."

Looking a bit embarrassed, Colton raked a hand through his hair and sighed. "You know we had to go all the way back to the far side of the structure, right?"

Jake nodded.

"We replaced all the rotted wood and with the new roof

going on, that solved the issue with where we believe the water damage came from."

"And?"

Colton cursed under his breath. "There was a safe in the wall. Must have been a secret one because we didn't see any access to it from the interior."

"A safe? You're freaked out over a safe?"

"Well...yeah," Colton replied, still looking uncomfortable. "Fell on Danny's foot and...I had Tom take him to the urgent care, but I know how accidents on the job are and I want you to know the guys were doing everything right! We had no idea there was anything in the wall, so..."

Unable to help himself, Jake laughed–an honest-to-goodness hearty laugh. Hell, he'd been expecting some sort of bad report from the engineers or something that was going to add on to the cost of the job or delay it. He'd take a secret safe in the wall any day of the week.

Well, except he hoped next time no one got hurt.

"Where in the room was it?"

"It was behind the bed. There was a picture over the spot, but you couldn't access it from there–it had sheetrock completely over it–no secret panel or anything. It's like someone put it in there and wanted to forget about it." He paused. "If I were to put a safe in a wall, I know I'd want to get at it from time to time. Whatever's in there, no one wanted to get to. Isn't that odd?"

Beyond odd. But then again, everything seemed like that lately especially where the Coleman family and its descendants were concerned.

"Keep me updated on Danny and point me in the direction of the safe."

"I had a couple of the guys put it around back by the

door to the basement. It's real heavy and rusted. Not sure how you'll get it open."

"Thanks, Colt." With a wave, he walked around the back of the house and found the safe. Crouching down, he dusted it off with his hands and wondered if there was anything inside. The addition was done maybe thirty years ago so he knew it was Zeke's doing, but...why had he never mentioned it? There were lots of little oddities with this house–secret room in the cellar, a moving bookcase in one of the upstairs bedrooms–but not once had he mentioned hiding a safe in the wall.

He stared at it for a long time and realized he needed to let Susannah know about it and then find some sort of locksmith or something to figure out how to open the damn thing.

So not what he needed right now.

Or...he could tell Susannah about it and let her handle it. Technically this wasn't part of the job and the safe was part of her house, so...it would be better to let her be the one to take care of it. Plus, it meant he could focus on other things like the other job sites in town.

Like the roof on the building next to Barb's Beach Buys...

Okay, maybe he had been thinking about going into town and looking around at that site because he wanted to make sure things were going all right. If it happened to be next to the place where Mallory spent the last several days then...it was just a coincidence, right? And if he saw her, he'd be polite–neighborly–and ask how things were going. There was nothing wrong with that. No one could misconstrue his intentions because he was merely asking how she was handling her new business.

Nothing untrustworthy about that.

Making his decision, Jake walked back around to the front of the house and up the front steps where he found Susannah talking with Colton. She was laughing at something he said, her hand was on his arm, and if he wasn't mistaken, Colton was blushing.

Jake came up short and thought, "Oh my gosh...are they...flirting with each other?"

Instantly, he shook his head to push that thought aside because...just no. They spotted him and seemed to move a little farther apart and that's when he knew they were definitely flirting. Clearing his throat, he looked at his foreman. "Did you tell Susannah what you found?"

"Uh...no," Colton murmured, looking down at his feet. "I thought maybe you should be the one to tell her."

Suppressing the urge to roll his eyes, Jake smiled at Susannah and told her about the safe and where it was found. "It's in the yard right now by the cellar door. You're going to need to find a locksmith or someone to open it unless you've found something that Zeke might have kept his records in and maybe a combination. I know you haven't gone through all of his personal effects yet..."

"Georgia and I are doing that next week," Susannah said. She was smiling but Jake could tell it was forced. No doubt there was going to be a lot of snark, sarcasm, and out-and-out fighting on that day.

He hoped he didn't have to be around to witness any of it.

Or at least that he'd be able to kick back with a bag of popcorn while he watched.

"Well, if you need help finding someone to help..." he began but secretly hoped she wouldn't take him up on the offer.

"I know someone who could probably help," Colton

said and Jake wanted to hug him for the save. He smiled at Susannah. "If you want, I can make some calls and let you know tomorrow."

The shy smile Susannah gave Colton as she thanked him suddenly made Jake feel as if he were some kind of voyeur and he excused himself.

And it didn't seem as if either of them even noticed.

For a few minutes, he walked around the property and pretended to be inspecting the work going on. It wasn't necessary. His crew were top-notch and they had been keeping him updated every day on the progress. There wasn't any need for him to be on site right now and that meant he was free to head into town and...

Groaning, he cursed himself for his lack of confidence and stormed off toward his truck. He climbed in and peeled out of the driveway with more force than was actually necessary.

The bad thing about living in a small town that was...well...small, was that he didn't have any time to really clear his head before he parked in front of Barb's shop. Spotting two of his workers up on the roof next door, Jake decided to go up and check on them first and see how progress was going with them.

Twenty minutes later he was back on the sidewalk without much memory of what his guys had even said to him.

"Jake?"

Turning, he found himself staring at Mallory and feeling a little stupid about being here. "Um...hey, Mal. How's it going?"

She wasn't smiling, but she wasn't frowning either. If anything, she was looking at him cautiously. "What are you doing here?" Then she must have heard the hammering and looked up toward the roof. "Oh, are those your guys?"

He nodded. "I'm making my rounds and checking on progress." Pausing, he wondered what he was supposed to say next. It felt ridiculous to be this nervous around her, but the last thing he wanted was to make matters worse than they already were. "So...uh...how are things going here at the shop? Things going okay between you and Barb?"

And then she seemed to relax a bit. "They're going well. Their system is woefully outdated so I know that is the first thing I'm going to have to look into. Other than that, I'm pretty excited to start learning the business a bit." With a small laugh, she went on, "But I have a feeling I'm going to be doing a lot of shopping for the house once I start looking at inventory and talking to buyers. It's going to be a real test of my self-control."

And he knew she was right. He remembered how much fun she had working on the boathouse all those years ago– she was a shopper extraordinaire and between the fun she was going to have with stocking the shop, she also had the house project to think about. More than likely, she was going to eat up her first month's profits in the blink of an eye.

"I'm sure your mother will keep you in line."

Shrugging, she replied, "Maybe."

Okay, he was done with small talk. Taking a step closer, he figured he needed to try to make things right. "Would you like to go to dinner tonight? We could go to Captain Bill's or if you're in the mood for Italian, we can go to Michael's. Totally up to you."

And then he held his breath nervously. He was completely expecting her to reject him and tell him it wasn't a good idea, and he had no words to convince her otherwise. At least, none that were coming to him at the moment.

"I'd like that," she said quietly. "Seven work for you?"

It was crazy, but he almost sagged to the ground in relief. "Yeah," he said, hoping he sounded casual. "That's good. I'll pick you up..."

Shaking her head, she said, "I'll just walk over to your place." Looking over her shoulder and then back to him, she told him she needed to get back inside and would see him later. It killed him not to kiss her goodbye, but he felt like things were still on shaky ground and didn't want to push his luck. "See you later."

Back in his truck, Jake did his best to focus on where he was supposed to go now and what else he had to do because all he wanted to do was go home and get ready for their date.

"Ugh...I'm pathetic," he grumbled as he drove down Main Street.

For the next several hours he did manage to focus on work—he checked on two additional job sites and then met with his lawyer and Richard McClellan to sign paperwork for the transfer of ownership of Coleman Construction. There were a lot of congratulations and handshakes, but when he stepped out onto the sidewalk after all was said and done, he felt oddly let down.

The feeling stayed with him the whole way home and through his shower once he got there. After he was dressed and waiting for Mallory, he couldn't shake it. This was something he'd worked for his entire life—to own a business like Coleman should have him feeling ecstatic.

And that's when it hit him.

This wasn't really his business. It was Zeke's.

He hadn't started it from nothing and built it up–Zeke had.

He was the owner of a successful business by default.

Muttering a curse, he walked to the kitchen and grabbed himself a beer. The last thing he wanted was for his mood to put a damper on his night with Mallory. After all, he needed to put things back on track with them and if he was distracted and moody, chances were he wasn't going to do much good.

Pushing open the back door, Jake stepped out onto the deck and walked out, leaning on the railing to stare at the Sound. It was beautiful out here–peaceful and relaxing and he forced himself to let some of the tension go.

Easier said than done.

Looking out at the water, he sighed. This was the life he wanted–to live and work in Magnolia and have it easier than his parents had. And now, thanks to Zeke, he would. However, now it made him feel like a fraud.

"Hey."

He turned at the sound of Mallory's voice. She was walking up the steps to his deck and had on a pale pink sundress and sandals. Just the sight of her took his breath away. Part of him was a little hesitant to go and kiss her like he normally would and instead he waited to see what she would do.

Stepping in close, she kissed him softly on the cheek and it made Jake feel like everything might just be all right.

"You were looking pretty fierce there," she said softly, leaning on the railing beside him. "Everything okay?"

And because he needed someone to tell him whether or not he was crazy, he told her exactly what he'd been thinking about.

Mallory looked at him thoughtfully for a long moment.

"You know that Pops didn't technically start Coleman Construction, right?"

"What?" This was brand new information. How could Zeke not have mentioned it in all of their conversations?

"His grandfather–my great-great-great-grandfather–was the one to do it way back at the turn of the century," she explained. "And with each generation, it has grown stronger and more successful." Then she smiled at him. "Just like it will for you."

"I don't know, Mal…"

"Maybe it's not the way you always dreamed it would happen for you. Maybe you thought you'd either start a company or buy one and take it over, but just because it didn't happen that way doesn't make this any less of an incredible thing for you! You're the new owner because you're the only one Pops trusted to take his company and make even more successful than he ever thought it could be."

"You don't know that," he said shyly, but her words were definitely making him feel better.

"Yes, I do," she countered. "I may have only spent summers here, but I spent enough of them sitting and talking with Pops that I can say with great certainty that he was pretty emphatic about who worked for him and who he trusted." She reached over and took one of his hands in hers. "He trusted you and believed in you more than he ever did with anyone else. So if you're having issues with this whole situation, the only thing I would suggest is kicking some major ass, taking the company to the next level and making Pops proud."

And when it was put like that, Jake knew he was crazy to doubt himself. Most people would love to be in his position and to have what he had. He was foolish not to be thankful. Leaning over, he kissed Mallory on the cheek. "Thank you."

"For what?"

Smiling, he wrapped an arm around her waist and pulled her in just a bit closer. "For always being willing to listen to me and talk to me." He kissed her forehead. "And for being exactly what I need."

She looked up at him with her big eyes and for the first time in days, he had hope for the future.

For them.

10

WHY WAS she fighting this so much? Right now, she had the ability to have everything she ever said she wanted so why wasn't she reaching out and grabbing it with both hands?

Leaving New York and her job to live in Magnolia Sound should be a no-brainer. Sure, Mallory loved her job, but most of her friends were married or had moved away so it wasn't like she had a raging social life to keep her there. Ever since she was a little girl she dreamed of moving to North Carolina and living here. Now that she had the best reason in the world to do it, though, she was hesitating.

Again, why?

The practical side of Mallory reminded her of the fact that she had job security up in New York. She did the work of three people and was in demand. Giving that up and moving here to run a beachy decorating shop didn't quite offer that same security. Mallory was the kind of person who thrived on having a good savings account, retirement account, and all that went with living within her means. To walk away from her 401(k)-providing job made her feel a little uneasy.

Sure she could leave the shop to run with a well-trained staff–one where they could handle the day-to-day operations. Then Mallory could stay up in New York and continue to work her full-time job. However, she'd have to come up with a plan where she'd come down and handle the bookkeeping, accounting, and ordering inventory once a month but...was that something she wanted to do? For starters, it would leave her no time to herself. She'd have to work extra hours every week so she could take the time off to come down here to see to the store. She knew that she'd be exhausted within a matter of months and somehow she didn't think that's what Pops intended for her.

Just thinking about the employment aspect of her life was enough to give her a headache.

And then there was Jake.

Throughout her teenage years, how often had she fantasized about having him as her boyfriend? It had been a dream that became a reality and then led to heartbreak. Now that they had finally talked about their breakup, Mallory knew it was for the best back then. It still hurt, but she was mature enough to know it happened for the right reasons.

Reconnecting with him–as a friend–was something she knew she'd do eventually, but this new turn in their relationship took her completely by surprise. Sure, she'd thought about coming back to town, having a steamy weekend of wild sex to get him out of her system, then leaving and happily moving on. Never in her wildest dreams did she imagine coming back and reconnecting as lovers who still had real feelings for each other.

And she did. She honestly and truly did. Hell, she'd never really stopped loving Jake. She was just so damn angry at the way things had ended between them. Now he was talking about forever but...Mallory wasn't sure she could trust what he was saying.

Because he had never said that he loved her.

Three simple words that would make all the difference in the world, but...he had yet to say them to her.

Ever.

It would be easy to convince herself that she didn't need the words–the feeling and the actions were there, right? But...she really wanted the words.

Okay, she really did need them.

On top of that, there was a tiny little voice in the back of her head that said this was all too easy. After six years, why did they suddenly get back together now? Was Jake simply looking out for her that night and they just fell back into a familiar routine based on their shared past? Did memories of their time together help them temporarily forget that they were grieving? And if that was the case, was what they were feeling right now even real?

"Why am I looking for trouble?" she murmured to herself. Jake was still inside sleeping and she was sitting out on the deck with a cup of coffee, watching the sun come up. It was one of her favorite times of day and she was kind of happy to be out here by herself.

Last night, she and Jake talked about so many things– they'd continued the conversation about his mixed emotions on inheriting the construction business but by the time they sat down to dinner, Mallory knew he was feeling better about it. Then they'd discussed her job back home and how her bosses were really anxious for her to get back. To his credit, Jake didn't try to persuade her one way or the other, but she knew what his preference was where her job was concerned. They talked about the renovations they needed to do on Pops' house to make it into the bed and breakfast and how she was going to utilize her newly-acquired shop to do most of the decorating. All in all, it was a wonderful night filled with great conversation and followed with amazing sex. It was everything that could be hers if she moved here and lived in Magnolia full-time.

She was getting nowhere. And the one person she would normally reach out to for advice was gone.

Yeah, she was starting to finally come to grips with the fact that Pops wasn't here anymore. She hadn't even read the letter he left her because doing so would make this all too real and permanent. It was something she'd do eventually, but right now her heart just couldn't handle it.

Taking a sip of her coffee, Mallory thought about the conversations she had with her mom and cousins in the last couple of weeks. At first, all of them were super excited at the thought of her moving back but then backed off. Was she giving off some sort of vibe where everyone sort of knew she wasn't going to do it? Was she subconsciously doing that?

Behind her, the sliding glass doors from the master bedroom opened and she turned to see Jake standing there in nothing but a pair of dark boxer briefs and her mind went completely blank.

Well, not completely...the word *yum* came to mind.

Without a word, he held out a hand to her and Mallory slowly walked over to him and took it.

A minute ago she was thinking about the direction of her life, but right now, the only thing she wanted to think about was giving Jake a morning to remember.

Was he tired? Yes.

Was he sore? Also yes.

Would he choose to start every day like this one? Hell yes.

It was safe to say that he and Mallory were back on track. Of course, that would be true only if back on track meant they talked about every topic under the sun except for her moving to Magnolia Sound for good.

It was barely noon and he was on his fourth cup of coffee, still exhausted mentally and physically. All night he had tried to get her to come around to his way of thinking without badgering her about it. He'd talked about the shop and how great she was going to be with it and gave her some suggestions on expansion and yet...nothing. She still talked about commuting back and forth to make it work and how hard she'd worked to get her promotion. Then he felt guilty about even wanting her to pick up and move here and sat back and listened as she waxed poetic about all the things she was looking forward to with her new position.

Did he come right out and ask her to move? No. Did he point out how grueling that kind of commute was going to be for her? No. Was he trying to be encouraging and supportive? Yes. And where did it get him? Nowhere.

"Jake! Can I talk to you for a sec?" Colton called out. He was back over at Susannah's because they were finishing up the deck today and waiting on inspections.

"Sure. What's up?" Walking closer, he saw his foreman looking a little more uncomfortable than usual.

Colton was rubbing a hand along the back of his neck and fidgeting a bit. "So um...the deck is done and the repairs on the addition exterior will be done by early next week."

This wasn't news to Jake so he nodded and waited.

"I was curious if...you know...if Ms. Westbrook made any decisions on starting work on the interior." He paused and gave a weak smile. "If she did, then it would be great if we could just plan on staying put and maybe I could go inside and start looking at where we'll be starting."

Oh, good lord…

He hung his head for a moment and shook it before looking Colton in the eyes. "So what you're saying is that you'd like to be the one heading up the next phase of this job, is that it?"

"Yes, sir," Colton replied with a curt nod.

"I see. And why would you want to? Interior work usually isn't your thing. You've often said how much you prefer working outside and dealing with major construction. This job is going to be pretty confining and more like carpentry at times. Seems to me you're a little over-qualified for it."

Okay, he was totally baiting the man, but it was a great distraction right now.

"Oh…uh…normally I do," Colton stammered. "But because this house is just so…you know…and it was Ezekiel's and he was always very nice to me…I think it would be a challenge and something different…and…it's historical so…"

"And seeing Susannah every day could be a perk," Jake threw out there.

"Exactly!" Colton agreed and then his hands instantly covered his mouth.

Taking pity on him and placing a hand on his shoulder, Jake said, "It's okay, Colt. I get it. You like Susannah. It's not a big deal."

Colton lowered his hands and let out a long breath as he shook his head. "That was really unprofessional of me. You need to put someone in charge of the renovation who is the most qualified and here I am asking to do it just so I can keep hanging around and getting to know Ms. Westbrook."

"I'm pretty sure she wouldn't mind you calling her Susannah..."

"Maybe, but I don't want to seem too forward. She's been really nice to me and I know she's grieving right now and I don't want to upset her by being rude or pushy or..."

"Honestly, I think being on a first-name basis with her would be okay. She's pretty laid back about that kind of thing."

Colton held up a hand to stop him. "Look, you're the boss and you do what's right for the client–Ms. Westbrook. I know I usually head up the commercial sites and I'll keep doing that because the last thing you need is to have to babysit me if I screw this up because I want to try something new. Maybe you could come by my place sometime. I just re-did my kitchen and it looks great and you could see if you like my work and maybe if you can't find someone who meets all the qualifications for this job..."

"Colton!" Jake snapped, unable to listen to another rambling word. "I get it. You want the job here and I have no problem with you doing it, okay? I'll set up an appointment for the three of us–you, me, and Susannah–to discuss the details, okay?"

He must have sensed how frustrated Jake was because after an overly-enthusiastic handshake, he thanked him a dozen times and quickly walked away. Jake didn't let out an easy breath until Colton was completely out of sight. If anyone would have told him that the craziest thing to happen on a job site was that he'd be dealing with a lovesick foreman, he would have laughed.

Although, all things considered, it was a pretty easy situation to deal with.

After that, he met with the inspectors for the deck and everything passed just like he expected. He led them around to the work being done on the addition and discussed the timeline for completion and when they'd need to come back to inspect that work as well. He took several phone calls and managed to handle some small crises without having to get in the truck and go anywhere.

With it being almost lunchtime, Jake thought he'd go and look for Mallory to see if she wanted to grab something to eat with him. He'd gone all of three steps when Marshall Browning, one of the city inspectors, started walking toward him.

"Hey, Marshall," Jake said, shaking the inspector's hand. "What can I do for you?"

"Nothing really," Marshall replied. "Everything's looking good here. I guess I just wanted to see what your plans are for Coleman."

"What do you mean?"

"Well, we all figured you'd be the one taking over when Zeke was gone, but I was curious if you were going to expand? Maybe move westward to the Piedmont portion of the state or even branch out to other states." He shrugged. "Zeke was pretty intent on staying here in Magnolia and the surrounding towns, but I figured you'd want to expand."

"I...I honestly haven't given it much thought..."

"Hell, you could probably do something up and down the entire east coast if you wanted to!" Marshall said with a big smile. "Could you imagine how proud the old man would be if you did something like that? See, if you ask me, Zeke didn't dream big enough. Everything he did, he did for this town and this town only."

"That's because his family founded this town," Jake

countered. "If you ask me, he took pride in that and it was a good thing."

"No, no, no, I get it. I'm just saying that it wouldn't hurt to do more! He was a smart businessman and maybe he could have impacted more towns and cities if he had tried."

At that point, Jake tuned him out. Zeke didn't want to do anything beyond Magnolia because this is where his heart was—always, right up until his dying day. There wasn't a damn thing wrong with that. But expanding? Could he really do that? *Should* he really do that? There would be a lot of research involved to see if it was the right thing for the company. It would give him the opportunity to put his own stamp on the company—something he had been struggling with. Could the solution really be this simple?

"You're young and you have a degree and there is just so much more you could do with this company, Jake," Marshall was saying. "I know this is all new, but you really should consider it."

"I might just do that."

"Oh, come on now. Don't be timid! Take control of your destiny! Make old Zeke proud!"

The phone rang and when he looked down at the screen, he knew he had a way to get out of this conversation with Marshall. "Marshall? Always good to see you, but I need to take this." He shook his hand. "Take care!"

Walking away, he answered the phone and listened to the project manager on the hospital job talk about the shortage of materials and knew he was going to have to take the ride into town to see what he could do. Chugging down the last of his coffee, Jake reminded himself of how much he loved this place and all the challenges that went with it. He knew he wouldn't give it up for anything in the world.

"Okay...I'm really doing this," Mallory said as she climbed from the car. She grabbed the picnic basket from the back seat and then stood and simply looked out at the landscape.

The cemetery.

With a fortifying breath, she slowly walked toward the newest gravesite while giving herself a pep talk.

"This isn't weird. There's nothing wrong with what you're doing. He may not be able to answer any of your questions, but...this was always our thing and I'm not going to stop just because..."

She stopped in her tracks and willed the tears not to fall. Memories of all the picnic lunches she and Pops had shared over the years came to mind and Mallory knew this was her way of honoring him–a tribute to their relationship–and she needed to pull herself together and do this.

Gently, she laid out the small blanket she had brought with her on the grass next to the freshly-packed earth. Sitting down, she pulled out her sandwich and fruit salad, a small container of cookies and a bottle of sweet tea. Letting out a long breath, she stared at the marker on the ground with Pops' name on it before she began to talk.

"So...I'm here," she began, hating the tremor in her voice. "Some people might think this is strange and that I'm maybe crazy for coming here like this but...this was our thing, right?" Tears stung her eyes and to distract herself, she reached for a cookie. Smiling, she looked at the marker. "You always said dessert before a meal was allowed so..."

Taking a bite of the chocolate chip cookie, she gave herself a minute to compose herself. "Here's the thing, Pops. I'm so sad–like seriously beyond sad. I miss you so much and I'm so sorry that I didn't come to see you this summer.

Looking back, it was incredibly selfish of me and now...now I'll never get that time back." She paused and gave up the fight on the tears and simply wiped them away. "I wish I could go back in time and make that decision over again. I know it's not possible but...there it is. The thing is, I know we talked and you told me you understood and I know you did, but it was still so wrong of me. I was being a brat and I'm just so sorry."

Reaching for her sandwich, she took a bite and cursed herself for being lame. She knew how much Pops always hated weakness and people who would snivel around looking for forgiveness or approval–the two things she was currently doing.

Swallowing her bite, she put the sandwich back down. "You knew it was your time," she went on. "That's why you wouldn't leave the house. I know you left this world exactly where you wanted to but you have to know you left a lot on the rest of us. Mom and Aunt Georgia are going to be fighting for a long time." Then she laughed. "Although I think you knew that and I hope you're able to see exactly how it all plays out."

Pausing, she took a sip of her tea. "And then there's Sam. He's so angry right now but...I think he's going to do the right thing. You always said you knew what was right for him if he'd only stop fighting and listen. I think he's ready to listen. Well, I hope he is. I think working in landscaping will give him the peace that he's never known. He's really good at it–as you obviously know–and I hope he has the confidence in himself to do this."

Shifting on the blanket, Mallory ate for a few minutes in silence. There was a light breeze and the large magnolia tree to the left of her offered the perfect amount of shade.

"I'm torn, Pops," she began again. "I worked so hard to

achieve what I have at my job and I finally got the recognition I deserve and...how am I supposed to just give it up?" Unfortunately, there were no answers, just the sound of birds chirping. "I think about working at the shop and helping Mom with the renovations and that excites me like you can't even believe, but once the house is done, is this really enough to keep me here?"

Isn't family enough to keep you here, computer girl?

Gasping, Mallory looked around because Pops' voice was as clear as day. It was the exact thing he would have said to her if he were sitting here himself. And, as would usually happen, his words had her thinking.

"Okay, yes. Being close to family would be great! I mean, everyone would be here–mom, Sam, all the cousins– but...they all have lives! Careers! Can I honestly have a fulfilling and satisfying career just working at the beach shop?"

Seems in my day women were happy to settle down with a man and have a family. Why can't that be fulfilling and satisfying?

She remembered a conversation they had many years ago when he said that exact thing to her and it made her think of Jake. If there was anyone she wanted to settle down with and have a family with, it was him. And if she could get past the whole omission of the "I love you" from him, she would seriously consider it.

Or maybe she shouldn't get too far ahead of herself.

But he did mention forever, so...

"Dammit, Pops!" she cried, slamming her hand on the ground. "This is just all too much! Why couldn't you have talked to me about this first? Told me what you were planning? Maybe if I had some advanced warning that you were considering leaving me the shop, I would know how I should have prepared!"

Even as she said the words, Mallory realized how unreasonable she was being. Pops did something wonderful for her and it wasn't his fault that she was having a hard time figuring out where she was supposed to be.

They have computers in Magnolia Sound, sweet pea. It's not just a New York thing.

And that was something she had been telling herself for the last several days. She'd be giving up her job with the company she had been with for two years to start over somewhere new. It wasn't the worst thing in the world, right? To be able to live where she always wanted to live and be near her family and Jake...well...wasn't that worth it?

There was another tiny voice in her head that wouldn't shut up, reminding her of how important it was to work hard and be successful. The constant chatter of how hard she'd worked for her degree and all the hours she'd put in to get to this point in her career, along with the prestige of getting this promotion...

Ugh...she wished that damn voice would just shut up!

Quietly, Mallory finished her lunch and then looked around her. Even the cemetery was beautiful. Everything was peaceful here and as much as it made her heart ache, she knew this was the perfect resting place for Pops.

She reached into the basket and pulled out the envelope Richard had given her the day the will was read. It was something she'd been avoiding, but now seemed like the perfect time to read it.

My sweet Mallory,

Boy this is some pickle, isn't it? I feel like I should be sitting under one of our magnolia trees holding your hand and talking to you rather than doing it like this. It doesn't feel right. One of my greatest joys in life was sitting and talking with you. You were always so smart and insightful, but more than that, you were more than happy to sit and listen to the ramblings of this old man. Thank you for letting me relive my glory days every time we sat down together.

You have grown into such an amazing young woman and I am proud to be your great-grandfather. I have to admit, I never understood all that crazy technology stuff you prattled on about, but you are passionate about it and I knew you'd make a success of yourself doing it. Just remember this—all the success in the world means nothing if you're alone. Your mother misses you, your cousins miss you, your brother needs you, but most of all, Jake needs and misses you. He don't say it much, but I can tell. Trust me, I never thought I'd be the kind of person to butt into other people's business but I just thought you should know that.

I know you're hurting and I know why. And I understand why you didn't come home this summer. I missed you, but I understood. I'm sure you're beating yourself up over it but that's not what I want. You're a grown woman who is entitled to have the time and space you need. You always called and we talked all the time.

By now I'm sure you know what I've left for you and I want you to know I'm not going to explain myself. All I'll say is that damn shop gave you so much joy every time you came to visit that I thought you should have it. As for what I left to Sam, well...promise me you'll keep an eye on him and convince him to work with it. He's not as smart as he thinks he is and I know a career change will be good for him. He never would listen to me but maybe he'll listen to you.

Sweet pea, remember all of our picnics. Remember holding my hand as I explained what all the flower names are. Sit out on the deck and enjoy the sounds of the waves.

Take time to watch the sunset. These are some of the things I never took for granted and I don't want you to either. Be happy in this life and know that I love you. And this isn't goodbye. We'll see each other again someday.

Love, Pops

Hugging the letter close to her chest, she cried anew. It was the most perfect thing he could have done for her and the fact that she chose to read it now made it feel like they were really having one of their picnics together.

"I miss you so much, you know. Every day. I walk around the house and I keep waiting to hear your voice. Then I go outside and look at the gardens and they're all torn up and I imagine seeing you working to put them all back together." She paused. "It's so hard when it hits me that none of those things are going to happen ever again."

She sat there for a long time before she started to pack things up. When everything was folded up and put back in the basket, Mallory stood and said a silent prayer. "I'll miss you every day. And I promise to do everything I can to make you proud," she said quietly. "I love you."

With her head hung low, she made her way back to her car and put the basket on the back seat. The drive through the small cemetery was done through a sea of tears. Before turning onto the main road, she took a minute to compose herself. Looking at herself in the mirror wasn't an option–she already knew she was a mess–but the only thing she wanted to do was get back to the house.

When she pulled in the driveway a few minutes later, there were construction vehicles everywhere. It wasn't anything new, but she really hoped to get into the house without anyone stopping to talk with her. Luckily she didn't see Jake's truck anywhere so she knew that was one less person she would have to deal with. Weaving her way around the workers, Mallory opted to go around the house and out to the yard. She glanced at the newly-completed deck and smiled before heading down to the pier and to the boathouse. Both still needed some minor repairs, but right now, she hardly noticed.

Once inside the boathouse, she turned on the small A/C unit, closed the shades and curled up on the sofa. This was her place–her little hideaway from the rest of the world. Exhaustion had her almost asleep as soon as her head hit the pillow. She kicked off her sandals and pulled the soft afghan that was draped over the back of the sofa over her as she curled up on her side. There would be time to think about work and job decisions later, but for right now, she just needed to rest her eyes and pretend the rest of the world didn't exist.

Whenever Mallory couldn't be found in the house, it was common knowledge that she was down in the boathouse. Jake had gone looking for her when he was done with work for the day and after both he and Susannah couldn't find her, he knew exactly where to go.

The property was finally quiet now that everyone was gone for the day and it felt good. Nice. Exactly the way things used to be before the hurricane blew through and turned life upside down. Jake made a note of the few boards on the pier that still needed to be replaced and when he reached the door of the boathouse, he lightly knocked so he wouldn't startle Mallory.

When he stepped inside, it was dim and cool and he could see her curled up, sound asleep on the sofa. Closing the door, he stepped closer to her and kicked off his shoes.

Unable to help himself, he crouched down in front of her and gently combed her hair away from her face. She hummed softly in her sleep and he could tell she'd been crying.

He rested his head on the edge of the sofa and sighed. Even though he had no idea what exactly had caused her tears, he was sure all the pressure she was under was part of it. And what was he doing? Adding to it. It didn't matter how much she kept talking about needing to go back to New York and her job, all he wanted was for her to give it up and come to live in Magnolia with him. And because he knew her family so well–and even though he asked them not to–Jake was pretty sure the rest of her family had been after her to make the move as well.

The thought of Mallory not being here with him every day made his heart actually hurt. He didn't want to think of a day without her, but...he also didn't want to see her looking this sad and exhausted. She deserved to have every-thing she wanted and to be happy, so if going back up north to her job is what did that for her, then...he would stand back and let her go. That didn't mean he was giving up on the two of them though. They'd deal with the long-distance thing and he'd help her with her business in any way that he could and he'd go up to New York and see her and then try to be patient and wait for her to come back once a month to handle the shop. It could work.

It had to.

Carefully, he crawled onto the sofa behind her and got under the blanket with her. Gently, he wrapped one arm around her and lined their bodies up in the way he knew she loved. Everything in him relaxed because just being close to her did that to him. For now, he simply enjoyed the quiet with her because once she woke up, he was going to encourage her to leave–to follow the dream she had worked so hard for and promise her that he'd be here waiting.

Then his conversation with Marshall came to mind.

Expansion didn't just have to be in the surrounding states, he could just as easily start up a branch of Coleman's up in New York as he could somewhere closer like Virginia! The idea had merit and maybe they could find a way to split their time between their two places and work their jobs and...it would be crazy and chaotic and a lot of time on the road, but it would all be worth it if at the end of every day, he could hold her like this.

As his mind began to swirl with ideas about expansion and traveling and all the possibilities, Jake couldn't help but yawn. The day was catching up with him and he promised to rest his eyes for just a few minutes before waking Mallory up and taking her to dinner where they could talk.

He placed a kiss on her shoulder and hugged her a little closer. And as his eyes drifted shut all he could think of was how he couldn't wait to tell her the great news for their future.

11

"You're going to *WHAT?*" Mallory cried later that night. She shook her head, certain she was hearing things.

"I'm going to look into opening a division of Coleman's up in New York!" he said excitedly. They were eating pizza out on his deck and he looked genuinely happy with the news he had sprung on her.

"Jake, it's crazy! You can't just start up another division of Coleman's! Just...no."

He looked at her in disbelief. "Why not? It's the perfect solution to everything!"

Tossing her pizza back down onto the box, Mallory mentally counted to ten before speaking again. "Okay, for starters, you're just now taking over the business and you have more than enough work here in Magnolia to keep you busy for the next year. Easily."

His expression told her he hadn't thought of that.

"Pops wasn't interested in branching out. It wasn't what was important to him. Now I get it that you're looking for a way to make the company your own–and I'm not saying you should never expand, but the timing just isn't right for you to do it this soon."

"Mallory..."

"And why are you suddenly so interested in this? Just days ago you were all about me moving here and working both jobs! Why the change of heart?"

He let out a long breath and put his own pizza down. "I realized how selfish I was being!" he snapped defensively. "When I went to the boathouse and found you, I could tell you'd been crying and it hit me how much you've had to deal with. Then I realized how much I was adding to your stress and thought this would make a great compromise." Raking a hand through his hair, he let out another long breath. "I thought this would make you happy, Mallory."

It hit her how much he was trying–trying to make things right for her and for them. It was a very plausible solution so she could have her cake and eat it too, only...it felt wrong. Not that he wanted to be with her, but that he was diving into an expansion because of her.

"Jake, it's...it's too much. You need to wait before tackling something like this," she said, feeling like she was being the voice of reason. But when Jake jumped to his feet cursing, she had a feeling he didn't see it quite the same way.

"Dammit, Mallory!" he yelled. "Do you even want to be with me or are you just killing time here?"

"Oh, my gosh...are we back to this again?" she said with exasperation. "I mean honestly, Jake, this is getting crazy! If I didn't want to be with you, I would tell you!"

"Then why is it every time I find a way for us to be together–for us not to have to do the long-distance thing–you back off or argue about what it is I'm trying to say or do?"

"I don't do that..."

"Yes, you do," he countered and then paced away before turning back to her. Walking closer, her gently grasped her shoulders. "Don't you get it? I want to be with you. The thought of you going back to New York and only coming back once a month to work at the shop is killing me! When I look at you, I see everything that I want–a future! But if you don't feel the same or if you don't want the same thing then...could you just say it now? Please?"

He was killing her. So much of what he was saying was exactly what she wanted. She loved him and...dammit, she wouldn't put her heart out on the line again and have him not do it. Sure he was saying things that sounded like he felt the same way, but Mallory needed the words–needed him to say it without her asking him to. Maybe it was petty and childish, but she'd learned the hard way that words did matter.

Knowing she had to be the voice of reason, she did her best to calm him down. "Jake, you know how much you mean to me, but things are a little chaotic right now. Why can't we just give this a try to see how it works–me coming back once a month and you working on rebuilding Magnolia Sound? You have more than enough to keep you busy and I know you say it will be hard for us not to see each other, but I think we'll have too much to do to focus on that." She offered him a smile but he didn't return it.

With a huff, she pulled out of his grasp.

"Look, I'm not saying it's going to be perfect, but shouldn't we at least try?"

She was expecting Jake to argue–to tell her she was wrong–but he didn't. Instead, he walked over and began cleaning up their dinner. Once he had everything stacked up and ready to bring into the house, he faced her. "If that's what you want, then that's what we'll do." His words were spoken so quietly that she almost didn't hear him, but the expression on his face said it all.

He would do this for her.

Just like he would have expanded his business to New York just so he could be with her.

Maybe words weren't his thing, but his actions–his sacrifices–said it all. Slowly, Mallory walked over to him and cupped his face in her hands. "Why?" she asked softly. "Why are you so willing to keep doing this?"

The last time she saw him look so overcome with emotion was the day of Pops' funeral. It almost broke her then, and it was about to break her now.

Jake mimicked her pose. His large hands holding her face. "Because I love you," he said gruffly. "I keep trying to do what I think will make you happy and…and it seems like I keep messing it up." He rested his forehead against hers. "So we'll do whatever it is that you want us to do and we'll make it all work because I'd rather have one week a month with you than nothing at all."

Tears fell in earnest before Mallory could even think to stop them. Closing the distance between them, she kissed him–kissed him with everything she had and melted against him as he kissed her back just as urgently. They moved together–banging into deck furniture as well as the side of the house in their attempt to get inside. At the sliding door, Mallory pulled back and smiled at him. "I love you so much," she said breathlessly. "Six years ago I fell in love with you and I don't think I ever stopped."

His knuckles caressed her cheek. "Six years ago I was too stupid to tell you how I really felt. I was afraid to believe that what I felt–what we had–was the real deal because there were so many damn obstacles. So I didn't say the words. I thought if I didn't say them, it would make things easier when it all fell apart." He placed a gentle kiss on the tip of her nose. "But it didn't. If anything, I've kicked myself every day for not being as brave as you."

She gasped softly. "You think I'm brave?"

He nodded.

"But...why? I'm a damn mess, Jake. I can't seem to make a decision about my life or what I'm supposed to do and..." Okay, it was time to put it all out there. If he could be honest, so could she. "I hated that you never said you loved me," she admitted lowly. "And not just six years ago. But since I've been back. Every time you talked about wanting me to move here and be with you, I kept waiting for you to say the words. I thought if you said them it would help me make sense of everything."

He gave her a lopsided grin. "And did it?"

She shook her head. "No. It didn't. And do you know why?"

Now it was his turn to shake his head.

"Because you proved to me every damn day how you felt and I was too blind to see it."

Jake hugged her close. "I think we need to get better about talking to each other. I've spent every day since you've been back thinking you didn't want to be with me and second-guessing myself. Promise me we'll do better. Remind me every day if I'm messing up."

Kissing his chin, she pulled back slightly and grinned up at him. "That's a lot of power you're giving me right there. You realize that?"

Chuckling, he hugged her even tighter. "You're not the type to take advantage of that. And...just so you know...I'll be sure to remind you if I think you're messing up so it will be fair."

"Hmm..." She snuggled in close, loving the feel of his

arms around her and the sound of his heartbeat under her ear. "I guess it's only right. But..."

"But...?"

"I don't think it will be necessary because we've got this. We've worked hard to get where we are and things are going to be crazy for the next several months, but it will all be worth it."

"Yes it will." Then he released her and took her by the hand. Mallory was certain they were finally going into the house, but they didn't. Jake led her across the deck, down the steps and across the yard. At the pier, he continued to lead her down toward the boathouse where they climbed onto the party deck. He sat in one of the lounge chairs and gently pulled her down onto his lap. "I like watching the sunset with you. Every time I came out here at this time of day when you weren't here, I would think of you." He kissed her and it was slow and sweet and wonderful. When he raised his head, he smiled. "That first night you were back, you were down on the pier and I thought I was seeing things–like my mind was playing tricks on me. So many times I imagined you standing out there in one of your sundresses watching the sunset. You always looked so peaceful and beautiful and..." He reached up and caressed her cheek. "Everything I ever wanted."

And those were the best words because he was everything she had ever wanted, ever since she was a teenager. Just knowing they were here together and in love like this made her believe that dreams could come true. She had never been a whimsical person, but right now, it was exactly how she felt.

They sat like that out on the deck until the sun was fully down. She was snuggled up in his arms and hated the thought of moving, but the promise of a comfortable bed being only a short walk away helped.

Slowly, she moved from his embrace and stood. "Come on, let's go home."

His smile was soft and full of gratitude as he came to his feet. "I like the sound of that, Mal. And someday, we're going to go to the same home together every day."

She really liked the sound of that.

"You guys really didn't need to do this," Mallory said for what felt like the tenth time. "I'm going to be coming back once a month!" They were sitting in massage chairs at Glitter Girls getting pedicures.

Peyton lifted her wine glass and smiled. "We know, but we wanted to have a little time alone with you before you left."

"Yeah," Parker chimed in. "Even though your plan sounds solid, we just figured you'd be busy catching up with Jake whenever you come back."

Yeah, it probably would be hectic at first, but hopefully it would get better. And once all the work on Pops' house was completed it would definitely free her up, which is what she said to her cousins. "I know it's not ideal, but... we're going to try and see how it goes."

"I don't get it," Peyton said as she got a little more comfortable in her chair. "All your life you talked about moving here and now that you have a legit reason to..."

"Several reasons to," Parker corrected.

Rolling her eyes, Peyton continued. "Several reasons to, why aren't you grabbing this with both hands? Why would you go back to New York where you'll be alone when you could be here with all of us? And Jake!"

"It's not that simple," Mallory explained. "Believe it or not, I worked hard to get where I am at work and I can't just walk away."

"I don't see why not," Parker commented. "Seems to me there are way more benefits for you to leave that job rather than stay."

"Parks," her sister gently scolded. "We're not supposed to be pressuring her, remember?"

Pouting a bit, Parker shrugged and took a sip of her bottled water. "I'd feel much better if I got to have some wine too, you know."

"And when you're twenty-one, you can," Mallory said, reaching over to pat her hand. "For now, you'll have to deal without it."

"Bummer."

They sat in companionable silence for a few minutes while their feet got pampered. The door to the salon opened and Mallory heard Peyton start to snicker. "What?" she whispered. "What's so funny?"

Leaning in close, Peyton said, "See that girl who just walked in?"

Mallory nodded.

"She's desperately trying to date Mason," she said with a laugh. "Like seriously trying to date him. She even made friends with my mother in hopes of getting fixed up with him."

"That's kind of sweet..."

But Peyton straightened and shook her head. "Trust me, it's not. She's a nightmare. I went to school with her and I am praying my mother sees through her and leaves my poor brother alone."

"I think Mason can handle himself," Parker said, her eyes closed as she enjoyed the foot massage she was getting. "You ask me and I'd say he's just about ready to hit his limit and personally, I can't wait."

"That's just weird, Parks, even for you."

She shrugged. "Mason has done whatever Mom and Dad ask of him because he didn't realize he could say no. With Pops dying, I think he'll take his inheritance and start branching out on his own."

"Oh, yeah!" Mallory said almost excitedly. "You guys never finished telling me what Pops left for Mason!"

Her cousins both laughed softly.

"Have you ever heard of The Mystic Magnolia?" Parker asked as she tried not to laugh.

"Um...no."

Peyton leaned forward. "It's a dive bar on the edge of town. Only locals go there and it's sort of a landmark."

"Yeah, for the senior citizen set," Parker added, finally letting herself laugh. "Like they all grew up going to this place and no one under the age of fifty would dare to go there!"

"So...Pops left your brother...a bar?"

Both her cousins nodded even as they continued cracking up.

For a moment, Mallory could only stare. It wasn't...the worst thing Pops could have done, but it was certainly confusing. Poor Mason. Clearing her throat and doing her best to keep a straight face even as her cousins were now both cracking up, she said, "So...does he know what he's going to do with it?"

"Mom wants him to sell it and is even looking for buyers for him," Peyton replied. "Mason has refused to get involved just yet. He claims he needs some time to think about it."

"What could he possibly have to think about?" Mallory asked. "He's not considering running it, is he?"

"Oh, gosh, no," Parker replied, resting back in her chair. "Maybe he's looking to make it an investment? It wouldn't be such a bad idea. Of course he'd have to put some money into it because the place truly is a dive. It's like an old shack that has another old shack attached to it." She shuddered. "I think the whole place should be knocked down and rebuilt. But that's just me."

"Personally, I think he should sell it, take the money and get the hell out of Dodge, you know?"

"Stop making it sound like leaving here is a good idea!" Parker cried. "Isn't that what you just got on me about?"

"This is different, Peyton, and you know it! It would be good for Mason to break free and have a life of his own without anyone poking their noses into his business!"

"Well, then you need to keep your opinion to yourself too! It's bad enough that he gets it al the time from our parents. So...just keep your mouth shut and see what he decides to do."

Leaning back in her chair, Mallory tuned her cousins out because she knew they bickered like this all the time. No one could ever convince her that leaving Magnolia Sound was the answer – even if it didn't seem like she was living that same philosophy. She wasn't leaving forever and the sooner everyone realized that, the better off they'd all be.

Including her.

***

Jake walked around the house and felt a little lost. He'd just gotten back from dropping Mallory off at the airport and even though they had talked about this ad nauseam, it was still harder than he thought.

Three months. They had decided to try living apart for three months. If at the end of that time they weren't happy, Jake was going to go up to New York and look into starting a division of Coleman's there. Mallory had tried to convince him that she should be the one to move to Magnolia but he knew how much her job meant to her and didn't want to see her make that sacrifice. Someday, he knew they would make their home here, but they had plenty of time to make that happen. She had never been shy about wanting to live in Magnolia, but the time just wasn't right for that to happen yet.

There was more than enough for him to do to keep him busy. Just...not right this minute. He was just about to sit down and turn on the TV when there was a knock on his back door. It seemed odd since no one was working next door at Susannah's and most people would have gone and rang the doorbell out front.

It was a bit of a surprise to find Sam standing there. Opening the door, he shook his hand. "Sam, hey. What brings you here?" Stepping in, Sam walked into the kitchen and seemed a little nervous. "Everything okay?"

"What? Oh, uh...yeah." He slid his hands into his pockets and motioned toward the living room. "Can we sit and talk?"

This was a bit odd, but... "Yeah, sure."

It took a minute before he started to speak. "So last night Mom and I finally got that safe open."

"Really?" he asked with surprise. In all the craziness of the last week, he had forgotten about that. "And?"

"And...there were some things in there. It was more like a time capsule than anything else."

"Wow. That's...that's interesting."

Sam nodded. "Anyway, we went through it all and sorted through pictures, newspaper articles and some other random stuff and found this."

He held out a photograph and Jake took it. It took him a minute to realize it was a picture of his parents and him standing with Zeke. Jake was a toddler in the picture–maybe two or three years old. Smiling, he looked at Sam. "Thanks. This is kind of cool. My folks took all the pictures with them when they moved but I don't think I've ever seen this one before."

"Read the back."

Brows furrowed, Jake turned the picture over.

*Jonah and Evelyn Summerford and my "great-grandson"
Jake*

How many times had Zeke told him he was family? And how many times had he wished it were true? He felt oddly emotional and the notation and when he looked up at Sam, he wasn't sure what to say.

"That was..." he paused. "Thanks."

Nodding, Sam stood and reached into his pocket and pulled out a small box. He sat and handed it to Jake. "After some discussion, we felt like this should go to you."

The box was definitely a jewelry box and he felt a little awkward taking it from Sam. When he opened it, he was beyond confused. "I...I don't...I mean...what is...why...?"

"Oh, right," Sam said with a chuckle. "I should probably explain." He shifted in his chair and grinned. "Okay, so that belonged to my great-grandmother. In this time capsule thing we opened, it stated that the ring should go to the eldest great-grandson. So..."

Jake had to think for a minute. "But...that's you, Sam. You're the oldest of Zeke's great-grandsons."

But Sam shook his head. "No, man. The picture says otherwise."

"Sam, seriously, come on. You can't...I can't possibly accept this. It's rightfully yours! A note on the back of an old photograph doesn't mean anything!" Jake tried to put the box back in Sam's hand, but he refused to take it.

Holding out a hand to stop him, Sam's smile faded. "Let me ask you something. Are you going to marry my sister?"

Holy crap.

"Yes," he replied confidently. "Yes, I am."

Sam grinned. "Does she know that?"

"I believe she does."

"Have you asked her yet?"

"Not formally, but...we've talked about our future and she knows she's the one I want to spend the rest of my life with."

Sam gave a curt nod. "Then that's why this needs to be yours, bro. You know Mallory was closest with Pops. We all know it. It makes sense that you should be the one to give her our great-grandmother's engagement ring."

"She might want one of her own..."

That made Sam laugh out loud. "Dude, you know my sister and this sort of thing is way more her style. Some women want a big, fancy engagement ring. But Mallory is going to love something antique that Pops had bought himself." He paused and his smile turned a little sad. "And you know Pops would love knowing that Mallory was wearing it now. So please...take the ring and when you guys make it official, give it to her. Show her the picture, tell her about the time capsule and just...trust me on this."

In a crazy way, it all made sense. Mallory wasn't impressed by material things and she preferred the senti-mental things in life. It would be the perfect ring for her and as he opened the box and studied the platinum band with the oval diamond, he knew she would love it.

"I don't know what to say," Jake said, looking over at Sam.

"Say you're going to take good care of my sister."

"Always, man. That's all I want to do."

"Then we're good here."

They sat in silence for a few moments before Jake asked, "Can I ask you something?"

"Sure."

"What would have happened if no one found the safe? Don't you think it's odd that it was hidden away like that? I mean, this ring is pretty damn important for Zeke to hide away like that."

"Yeah, Mom and I thought about that too but it turns out we would have found it eventually."

Now he was back to being confused. "How?"

"In Mom's inheritance for the house, Pops told her about it–about the safe. He hid it in the wall the way he did so no one would find it and try to steal the ring. We kind of think he was hiding it from Aunt Georgia, but we can't be sure," he added with a laugh. "Either way, we may have found the safe in an unconventional way, but what we found inside is now exactly where it belongs."

"This has all been so crazy. I swear Zeke was too crafty for his own good."

Sam nodded in agreement. "Tell me about it."

"You going to be okay? I know you aren't thrilled with what he left you..."

Waving him off, Sam came to his feet. "I'll be fine. I refuse to let Mason or anyone gain from it so I'll do what I have to do." He shrugged. "I can deal with living here for a year. It's not like I'm living the dream up in Virginia. My job does kind of suck so I'll do this for a while before I move on to the next thing."

"You never know. You may enjoy it! Seems to me that you haven't found a career to settle into yet. This could be it."

But Sam shook his head. "It's not the business that I'm against."

"Then what?"

"Do you know why I live in Virginia now rather than back up in New York where I grew up?"

Jake shook his head.

"Anonymity," Sam stated. "I know I've done a lot of stupid things in my life and if I'm ever going to be able to move on from them, I need to be where no one knows who I used to be."

"I don't think it's that bad, Sam. We've all done stupid things. Hell, I grew up here and we both know I was no choirboy."

Sam chuckled. "Are you kidding? You're the golden child of Magnolia Sound." Then he let out another laugh. "Well, you and Mason."

That made Jake laugh. "Thanks."

"You know what I'm saying. I'm not saying I did anything so horrific, but...I'm not proud of most of it and I would just prefer to live somewhere I've created a fresh start."

Jake stood and didn't know what to say. He knew why Zeke left Sam the landscaping business and how he hoped he'd stick with it. Maybe over the next year he could encourage him, but for now it seemed best to simply let him talk. "Sounds like a plan."

"I need to get going. There's a delivery of new shrubs

coming tomorrow and I have to finish clearing the beds in the yard." He shook Jake's hand. "I'll see you around."

"Take care, Sam."

And when he was gone, Jake collapsed on the couch and stared at the ring in his hand. It really was the perfect ring for her and he said a silent prayer of thanks to Zeke. It sucked that right now Mallory was flying home because more than anything, he wanted to propose to her right now and slide the ring onto her finger. They had a month before she would be back. After much discussion, they agreed that he wouldn't fly up to see her on the weekends or anything because she needed to get caught up on her work. It killed him to agree to it, but...he wanted to respect her wishes.

If he didn't, she would definitely remind him of it.

He missed her already and knew if he sat around like this much longer, he was going to go crazy. So he decided to head into his office and bury himself in work for a while.

A week later, Jake was dealing with the realities of being a full-time business owner. He wasn't used to being in the office quite so much, but it was becoming obvious that he couldn't be as hands-on on the job sites as he used to be.

And he wasn't sure if that was a good thing or a bad thing just yet.

His desk phone buzzed and he picked it up. "Mr. Summerford, your one o'clock is here," his assistant Julia said.

Looking down at his calendar, Jake didn't see anyone's name written down or that he had an appointment.

"Uh, Julia, I don't have anything written down for today. Are you sure they're here for me?"

"Yes, sir," she said pleasantly. "Are you sure you just didn't forget to write it down?"

That was always a possibility, but as he pulled up his calendar on his phone, Jake was certain he didn't have...

Office supplies. 1:00

Well, damn. Hard to argue with Google calendars, right?

"Why am I dealing with office supplies?" he asked. "Isn't that more of an office manager thing? Is Maggie coming in for this?"

"She's at lunch, sir. And no, this is something you need to look at first and then–if need be–we can set up a time for Maggie to follow up."

That seemed logical, but he still wished he was on a site somewhere hammering something. "Okay, fine. Send them in."

He hung up and fidgeted at his desk wondering what he was supposed to know about office supplies. Zeke never seemed to do this sort of thing, so why...

"Good afternoon, Mr. Summerford."

That voice.

Looking up, he saw Mallory standing in the doorway with a very sweet-yet-devilish smile on her face. Slowly, Jake came to his feet. "What...what are you doing here?"

She stepped further into the room and closed the door behind her. "It occurred to me that Coleman Construction is using an outdated and inefficient computer system."

It was then that he noticed the pencil skirt, the button-down white blouse, briefcase, and the stiletto heels. His girl was in business mode and it was sexy as hell. Quirking a brow at her, he asked, "Is that right?"

"Please, have a seat and let's talk," she said and Jake did as she asked. He figured she'd sit in one of the chairs facing him, but instead, she followed him around the desk and stood beside him. "It has come to my attention that the last time a new system was put in place here was five years ago. Is that correct?"

Honestly, he had no idea but he nodded out of curiosity.

"I know this because I assisted the management team with the installation at the time," she went on. "Knowing what I know now, that program is pretty much outdated and almost obsolete. It would be very beneficial to you–as a business owner–to update and install a new system now."

He was distracted by the way the buttons on her blouse seemed to strain against her breasts. It took a real effort to look up at her face–and when he did, he caught the knowing smirk she was giving him.

Clearing his throat, he questioned, "And I should just trust that you know what's best for this company?"

She nodded. "Absolutely. You see, I was very close with the previous owner and I'm even closer with the new owner, so..."

Slowly, he reached out and banded an arm around her waist, pulling her in close. "I'm the new owner," he said gruffly.

Smiling down at him, she said, "Then you know how close I am with you."

She smelled so good and was warm and soft and...

Standing, he couldn't wait any longer to kiss her. His hands raked up into her hair and with her heels on, she was almost his height. It felt new and different and yet absolutely perfect. She hummed as he kissed her and it was all he could do not to clear his desk and lay her down on it.

Mallory broke the kiss first and gave him a very triumphant look. "So what do you say, Mr. Summerford?

Are you ready to do a system overhaul with me?" she asked, her voice all sexy and sultry.

Was it wrong that he was totally digging this sexy executive vibe she had going on?

"Baby, I'm ready to do whatever it is you want," he growled before diving in for another kiss. He hated how they were in his office. In a perfect world there wouldn't be anyone on the other side of the door and he could take her right now like his body was almost demanding he do.

He kissed her until he couldn't breathe and then forced himself to pull back. Her skin was flush and she was panting and she was just...she was everything.

"What are you doing here?" he finally asked. "We said a month."

Licking her lips, Mallory smiled at him. "As soon as the plane took off, I knew I was making a mistake." She stepped away and rested a hip on the corner of the desk. "I loved my job but...it's just a job. My life, my future, is here with you."

"Mal, we talked about this. I would have moved, we would have made it work!"

But she shook her head. "It wouldn't have been right. This is where I always wanted to be and this is where you– and Coleman's–belong."

He didn't even know what to say. She was amazing and way more reasonable and practical than he could ever be. "So what does this mean? Are you...are you here for good?"

She nodded. "I am. I would have been here much sooner, but I sold off a lot of my furniture and then hired a moving company to get the rest down here. I know we didn't talk about this and maybe I made assumptions, but..."

He silenced her with another kiss. "No assumptions. I never wanted you to go," he said in earnest. "This is where you belong, Mallory. And whatever it is that you want to do–whether you want to stay with your mom or move in with me–it's still going to be the best thing in the world."

Her smile was that mix of sweet and sexy that she did so well. "I have a lot of stuff arriving here in four days. I don't know how we'll make it all fit, but..."

"I'll build an extension on the house if we need to," he countered with a laugh, unable to believe how happy he was at this moment.

With wide eyes, she hugged him. "I don't know if we need to go that far..."

"Doesn't matter. I want the house to be ours so we can wake up and look at the Sound or go down and sit on the deck of the boathouse and watch the sunset. That's where I want us to be."

"And that's where I want us to be. Forever."

No words have ever sounded sweeter.

"Have you eaten yet?" he asked. "What do you say we go have some lunch and you tell me how you managed to pull this off without me finding out?"

With an impish grin, she took him by the hand and led him toward the door. "You forget, I know the staff here pretty well. They've all watched me grow up. As soon as I told Julia I needed to surprise you, she came up with the appointment approach. Luckily she had access to your Google calendar."

He chuckled. "Very sneaky."

She laughed. "I know, right?" When they walked out to the reception area, Julia gave them both a wide smile and wished them a good day.

Jake didn't bother to ask where she was parked. He took the lead and got her into his truck and drove them home.

To their house.

It felt good to know it was finally happening. Which is what he told her.

"Finally? I've only been gone a week!" she said with a giggle.

"It's been longer than that." Reaching across the seat, he took her hand in his. "Six years, Mal. And I'm so happy it's happening now, but I want you to know I would have waited however long you needed. You know that, right?"

She moved closer and rested her head on his shoulder. "I do, and I love you for it."

When they pulled into his driveway, she looked at him curiously. "I thought we were going to grab some lunch?"

He put the truck in park and grinned at her. "We'll have some sandwiches." He paused. "Later."

And as she squealed with delight and climbed out of the truck, Jake knew life with her would never be dull.

"I'll race ya!" she called out, kicking off her shoes so she could run toward the back of the house.

Nope. It wouldn't be dull at all.

Looking heavenward, he smiled. "Thanks, Zeke."

Then he took off after his girl.

EPILOGUE

Two weeks later...

"Did you see that? It was a shooting star!"

Beside her, Jake yawned. "Was it?"

She nudged him with her elbow. "You're not even trying to pay attention," she said with a pout. They had eaten a late dinner out on the boathouse deck and the air was cool but it was a perfectly clear night for stargazing.

"Mal, we've been up since five this morning and painted half the house, moved furniture, and unpacked like a hundred boxes."

Now they were lying on one of the oversized lounge chairs on the deck and she knew it would be fairly easy to fall asleep right here. Not that it was a bad idea but...she really liked their bed back at the house.

With a dramatic sigh, she went to sit up. "Fine. I get it. You're exhausted so we should clean up and head in."

"Sounds good."

They stood and Mallory walked over to the table, began

clearing the dishes and putting them back into the cooler bag she used to carry them all out here. The whole table was cleaned and wiped down when she realized she'd done it all herself. "Honestly, Jake, if you're not going to help..." She turned around and froze.

He was behind her on one knee.

"Mallory Westbrook," he began softly.

"Oh my gosh, what's happening?" she said as her heart beat like mad in her chest.

Smiling, Jake reached out and took her hand in his. "Six years ago, you surprised the heck out of me when we collided in Zeke's living room. You had grown into this beautiful woman and I was a little ashamed to find myself having such a strong reaction to you." He paused. "Then you went and shocked me to my core when you kissed me. Never in my wildest dreams did I imagine that you had feelings for me." Then he smiled. "But I'm so glad you did."

She couldn't help but laugh softly. "You weren't saying that at first."

"I know. It's true, but...in my defense, you were so young and I didn't think I was good enough for you."

"Good thing I persisted. And for the record, I'm not *that* much younger than you."

"Are you going to let me do this?" he asked with just a hint of annoyance.

She nodded. "Go ahead. Sorry."

He squeezed her hand. "You were definitely persistent and I'm so glad you were. I never knew I could feel like this—that I could love this much. We traveled a long and bumpy road to get here, but honestly, I wouldn't change a thing. I appreciate who we are and all we have more than I thought possible. When I think about my future, it's with you. All of it. The good, the bad, and the bumpy." He gave her a lopsided grin before releasing her hand and opening the small box he was holding in his other hand.

"I love you, Mallory. And I want to spend the rest of my life with you." His hand trembled as he held the box up a little higher. "This ring..." he stopped and cleared his throat. "This ring belonged to your great-grandmother and Zeke passed it down to his eldest great-grandson."

"But...that would mean..."

Jake explained about the safe and the contents and then about the picture with the inscription.

"We all agreed that there is no one else in this world meant for this ring other than you. Will you marry me?"

Slowly, she dropped to her knees and kissed him. "Yes," she whispered against his lips. "Yes, I will. It's all I ever wanted. *You're* all I ever wanted."

He smiled and took the ring from the box and slid it onto her finger. "I always want to be the one to do that for you, Mal. To give you what you want, what you need. Always." He kissed her hand. "I love you."

"Let's go home," she said, "and celebrate properly."

The smile on his face told her he knew exactly what she meant. But as they stood, he gave her a counter-offer. "Or... we can go downstairs and stay in the boathouse tonight and remind ourselves where this all began."

And just like that, her heart melted. She reached out and caressed his cheek. "How did I get so lucky?"

"I'm the lucky one. You were the brave one and Zeke's birthday will forever be a reason to celebrate."

She looked at him oddly.

"That's the night of our first kiss. The night where we began." He kissed her hand. "The greatest night of my life."

Yeah, her heart definitely melted. "Then let's go downstairs and celebrate that night and all the other great nights–including this one."

"And all the ones to come."

PREVIEW OF: A GIRL LIKE YOU

CHAPTER ONE

"I'M IN HELL."

"Dramatic much?"

Sam Westbrook glared at his twin sister Mallory. "It's not dramatic, it's a fact."

Mallory rolled her eyes at him even as she smirked. "Care to clarify, then? Because from where I'm sitting, your life is pretty damn sweet."

Now it was his turn to roll his eyes. "Okay, if anyone needs to clarify anything, it's you. How could you *possibly* think my life is sweet? Look around, Mal! This is not my life! This is like some kind of nightmare!"

The look she gave him said it all–and yeah, he really was being dramatic. Sam knew he was being unreasonable, but this *really* wasn't the life he wanted for himself. This was a life that had been forced on him and he was marking the days on the calendar until he was free to go back to the way things were. To the life he had made for himself.

Only two-hundred and seventy days to go.

"Sam, you have got to get over it and move on. If you stopped being so angry, you'd see that your life here is really great. The business is doing well, the town is rebuilding which is helping the business grow, the work on the house is coming along and it looks great, we're all together so you're surrounded by family..."

"Mal, I think you're listing the reasons why *your* life here is great," he grumbled.

Mallory stood and slapped him on the back of the head on her way to the refrigerator. Reaching in, she grabbed two bottles of water, handing Sam one. "Why are you fighting this so hard? You're making more money than you ever have, you're living rent-free, I mean...think about it! There are worse situations to find yourself in."

"Maybe."

"No, not maybe. Definitely!" She sat back down beside him at the kitchen table and smiled.

He couldn't remember the last time he felt like smiling.

Oh, wait, yes he could! It was almost six months ago–right before Hurricane Amelia ravaged the east coast and destroyed not only a large portion of the small town of Magnolia Sound, but also their family. The storm may not have directly killed his great-grandfather, but the fact that their family patriarch perished during the storm didn't lessen the blow. When Ezekiel Coleman died, it left a big hole in all their lives. Within a week of his death, Sam found out his great-grandfather had left him a landscaping business–the biggest one in Magnolia Sound. Most people thought it would be a dream come true for him, but they were wrong.

So very wrong.

Did Sam enjoy working with plants and trees and shrubs? Yes.

Did he love being outside and making his own hours? Yes.

Did he want to be stuck here in this small, hick town for the rest of his life? Hell no.

Growing up, he'd spent most of his summers here and had developed a reputation for being a hell-raiser–and he had been proud of it at the time. Now? Not so much. Unfortunately, no one around here seemed to forget anything and no matter where he went or what he was working on, there was always someone ready to remind him of all his past transgressions.

So much for people deserving a second chance.

Mallory placed her hand on his and it broke him out of his reverie. "I wish you would give this a chance."

"I have!" he said a little too loudly. "You know I have, but the good people of Magnolia don't seem to want to ever let me forget all the shit I pulled when I was just a kid!"

"Sam, it wasn't that long ago when you admitted you almost got caught peeing in the church parking lot!" she reminded him with a small laugh. "You were hardly a kid and you knew better!"

Okay, so maybe he hadn't been trying all *that* hard to morph into an upstanding citizen, but still...

"Whatever," he murmured, slouching in his seat and raking a hand through his hair in frustration. "All I know is I have nine months left before I have my freedom back. Then I'm free to sell the business and go and do my own thing."

"You know that would break Pops' heart."

Yeah, he knew that and he didn't particularly like it, but Sam was also a little pissed that Pops had put him in this position in the first place. Getting the inheritance wasn't a bad thing, but the stipulation that Sam stay in Magnolia and work it for a full year was. And if Sam refused to follow those rules, he'd lose the business to his cousin Mason.

Unbelievable.

"He knew exactly what he was doing, Mal," Sam reasoned. "He knew he was forcing me to stay in one place and play by his rules–rules I never was very good at following. But I'm doing the right thing by him for the next nine months. After that, according to his will, I am free to do with the business whatever I want."

"I wish you'd reconsider."

"And I wish we weren't having this conversation, so..."

She let out a loud and overly dramatic sigh. "Want to come over for dinner tonight? I know mom's going out with Colton, so if don't want to be here alone you're more than welcome to join me and Jake. We're just grilling some steaks if you're interested. And it will be an early night since it's a Wednesday and Jake has to get up early for work tomorrow, so..."

And that was another reason Sam resented being here–everyone had a social life but him.

Correction - a *romantic* social life.

Since he'd never stuck around very long in the past, he was fine being a little of the love em' and leave em' type. Now that he was living here full-time? Uh, yeah...that wasn't going to work out too well for him and it certainly wasn't going to help his reputation.

As he found out after the first month here. How was he to know Rhonda and Kim were sisters? Yeah, it had been an extremely awkward night and he'd been lying low for a while ever since. Well, he'd been lying low here in town. He'd managed to convince Mason to drive down to Wilmington with him a couple of times so he could find someone to hook up with who he wasn't going to run into while out on his landscaping route.

It was exhausting and it was far too constricting of a lifestyle for him.

At first he had seriously considered turning down the inheritance and just letting his cousin have it, but after he had calmed down Sam knew that was the coward's way out. He had been given three months to get his stuff in order back in Virginia before he had to officially take the help of Coleman Landscaping. Quitting his job hadn't bothered him–it was just one in a long line of jobs he'd had in the last several years that bored him–but it hadn't taken long for him to realize there wasn't much holding him to his life there either. Sure, he had buddies he hung out with, but saying goodbye to them–even temporarily–really hadn't phased him all that much.

That wasn't normal, was it? Was he some sort of sociopath that didn't have any real feelings toward people? Or was it strange how he never developed any kind of attachment to a job or a place? Holy shit, what if something was seriously wrong with him?

"Earth to Sam!"

Oh, right. He was in the middle of a conversation. Clearing his throat, he decided to get off the topic of himself and on to another awkward one. "Does it bother you that mom is dating?" he asked his sister.

She shrugged. "It was a little weird at first, but...I don't know. This is the happiest I think I've ever seen her, and Colton is a really nice guy."

Sam couldn't disagree. "It's a little annoying how Mom's got a more active social life than I do."

"And whose fault is that?"

He shook his head and reached for his bottle of water. "This town's!"

"Oh, my gosh, are we back to that again? For the love of it, Sam, let it go! You did a lot of stupid things and now you have to prove to everyone that you've changed! It's not a big deal."

"Why should I have to?" he argued loudly. "I don't stand around passing judgement on everyone, why do they get to do it to me?"

"Not everyone is..."

"Oh, please," he interrupted. "Everyone is so damn uptight around here it's almost painful."

"Not true," Mallory said with a soft sigh. "You are completely over-exaggerating, and you know it."

Leaning forward, elbows on the table, Sam smirked. "Mal, you and I both know that no matter where I go, people give me looks." When she went to comment, he cut her off. "Old Mrs. Whitman at the grocery store? She always shakes her head and gives me a disapproving look when I go in there."

"You stayed out all night with her daughter Penny the summer we were seventeen!"

"She needs to move on! Penny's married with three kids!" Shaking his head, he continued. "Then there's Mr. Jenkins at the bank. I do all my personal and business banking there and he still acts like he doesn't want to touch my money."

"I'm sure you're exaggerating," she began and then her eyes went wide. "Oh, wait! You dated his daughter that same summer! When Penny was grounded, you took out *his* daughter! Her name was Jen or Jan or something like that."

Groaning, Sam hung his head.

"So the parents of this town aren't too fond of you. Some of them have a good reason."

"It's not just the parents. That uptight librarian is always looking at me funny too. Like she peers at me over her glasses like she's disapproving of something or other."

"When do you go to the library?"

"I don't!" he cried. "But I take care of the property next to it and whenever she sees me out there, I get the over-the-glasses glare."

Mallory studied him for a moment. "Wait. You mean Shelby? You know she's..."

"Doesn't matter." He shrugged. "I don't know what her name is. All I know is she's definitely got some kind of stick up her butt about something."

"Sam, Shelby's our age. Are you sure you didn't hook up with her and never call her again?"

"Dammit, Mal, it's not always that! I'm telling you, the people of this town are the worst!"

He knew his twin well enough to know she was carefully considering her words and mentally counting to ten before she spoke. After a minute, she looked at him serenely. "While I am sure there are some residents here in Magnolia who aren't the nicest people, I can't think of one who has gone out of their way to make a spectacle of themselves like you seem to thrive on doing."

"I haven't in a long time!"

"A long time? Really? Do you realize you're the reason there is a "No Public Urination" sign next to the church? Pastor Steve was devastated that he had to put it there!"

He didn't mean to snicker, but...it just sort of slipped out. When Mallory shot him a sour look, he instantly sobered. "Yeah, he's really the worst for sitting and passing judgement and really, he shouldn't."

"Oh, this I've got to hear," she said, her voice dripping with sarcasm.

"As a pastor, isn't it his job to preach forgiveness and not judging others? Isn't that biblical or something?"

The look she gave him said she agreed with him, but he knew she wouldn't say it out loud.

"So him and his secretary..."

"His wife," Mallory corrected.

"Whatever. So him and his *wife* look at me with those pinched expressions like their sucking on lemons or something, and yet he continues to call and ask for estimates on working on the church grounds." He paused and took a sip of water. "I mean, why? He clearly knows it was me so...is he just trying to bait me into coming to the church so he can yell at me? Condemn me? Pray for me?"

She rolled her eyes.

"If you were me, would you go there? Knowing how he felt about you?"

"For starters, I never would have done what you did."

Now it was Sam's turn to roll his eyes. "Yeah, yeah, yeah...you're perfect. Can we just *pretend* for a minute? Put yourself in my shoes?"

"Sam..." she whined.

"C'mon, Mal. Humor me."

She let out a long breath. "Okay, fine. No. I probably would not go there."

Her answer pleased him greatly.

"However..."

So close...

"You *could* send one of your top guys over to talk to Pastor Steve. You wouldn't have to do it yourself. It could be a good contract for you and good for the business. As a businessman, can you really afford to turn down jobs just because you're embarrassed by your previous behavior?"

And that was the thing with Mallory–she had a way of putting things into perspective that made complete sense and he couldn't argue with. The work the church needed was fairly extensive. They were going to take down a bunch of trees and create a small park on the church property and wanted Sam to do all the landscaping–including designing the space.

Apparently, someone had let it be known that Sam had some skills in that department and now they were interested in having him design something custom for them.

Ugh...why me?

"I guess I'll think about it," he murmured.

Mallory sat up straighter and smiled. "Excellent!"

And now he just wanted to move on to another topic. "So what else is going on with you? Anything exciting?"

"Not really. Wedding plans are at a standstill until we can get the work done here. I'm too afraid to set a date and then risk having the house unfinished."

He laughed softly. His sister had a weird obsession with this house–she had ever since they were little kids. It was their great-grandfather's home and had been in the family for over a hundred years and while it was nice, he never felt the connection to it that Mallory did. With their mother inheriting it and deciding to turn it into a bed and breakfast, there were a ton of changes it was going through, and she still was mildly obsessed with it. "Your fiancé is the contractor for the entire job, Mal. Surely he knows when the house will be done."

"You would think," she muttered and instantly cleared her throat and put a smile back on her face. "Jake and the crew aren't the problem. Mom is."

"What?" he asked with a laugh. "How is that possible? She's been very hands-on with the whole thing and all she does is talk about the work that's going on and how happy she is!"

"Sure, she's happy, but she also keeps changing things!

Half the original plans have been scrapped because she's come up with a better idea. She's making Jake crazy and she's frustrating me because it's always been my dream to get married in this house. The longer she drags this out, the longer I have to wait!"

"Maybe that's her plan," he teased. "Maybe she's not really on board with you marrying the boy next door, ever think of that?"

Mallory's eyes went wide and she paled. "Do you...I mean...do you think that could be it? I always thought she was okay with me and Jake and our relationship. There was a time when it was a little awkward, but...

Instantly, Sam felt bad for teasing her. Reaching out, he placed a reassuring hand on hers. "Mal, relax, I'm just messing with you. Mom adores Jake and we're all happy for the two of you. Seriously, I was just kidding around."

She practically sagged to the floor with relief. "Not funny, Sam!"

"Come on. It was a little bit funny."

She stuck her tongue out at him. "No, it wasn't. And just for that, I should invite Pastor Steve over for dinner to talk to you tonight!"

"You wouldn't dare!" But he saw the twinkle in her eye and knew she was just trying to get even. His sister was many things, but she wasn't mean and she wasn't spiteful.

She was the angel to his devil.

"You're right," she said with a pout, "but I really wish I could!"

"Nah, you're too nice." He took another drink of water. "So what else has mom changed?"

Standing, Mallory waved him off. "We'll talk about it tonight over dinner. Be over at seven and bring some wine."

If a bottle of wine was all it was going to take to get a free dinner, Sam was completely on board.

"I think I'm in a rut."

"No kidding."

Shelby Abbott rested her face in her hands and sighed. "No need to agree so quickly."

"Shell, I'm not trying to offend you…"

"Could've fooled me." Okay, she was being a bit of a drama queen right now, but when your best friend basically agreed with how pathetic your life was, it didn't quite inspire warm, fuzzy feelings. Tilting her head, she looked over at the one person who knew her better than anyone. "So what do I do, Laney? I am desperate for something… something exciting to happen to me! Something! Anything!"

It was late Friday afternoon and they were sitting in the break room in the library. Their shifts were over, and they had come back here to collect their things and ended up talking.

Well, Shelby had started talking and Laney had just sort of sat and quietly listened. Why? Because she was a good friend. The best, actually.

"If you really want to get out of this rut, you're going to have to venture out of Magnolia once in a while," Laney said, her tone wasn't the least bit condescending and yet she certainly got her point across.

"And go where? And why? What is so great about other towns that I have to go there to have some fun?"

Laughing, Laney stood up and walked over to pat

Shelby on her shoulder. "You've lived here your entire life and you have to ask that question?"

"Well...yeah."

With a sigh of her own, Laney walked around the table until she was facing Shelby. "This town is full of the people we've known all our lives. No one ever moves here! It's the same people, the same faces, the same stories! Gah!" she cried out. "Don't you want to meet someone new? Someone who doesn't know you were Miss Mini Magnolia in the second grade? Or how you had the chicken pox in middle school?"

"Maybe..."

"No maybes about it! Do you know how big the world is, Shell? Or even...just how big North Carolina is? There is so much to see and do and you never want to go anywhere! Why?"

Good question.

"I...I guess I'm just always busy," she said somewhat lamely. "The library keeps me busy and you know my folks always have something going on that they need help with..."

"Shell, it's time for you to start living for *you*," Laney said seriously, solemnly. "You need to have a social life. When is the last time you even went on a date?"

Ugh...she didn't even want to think about it.

"I don't know."

Laney placed both her hands on the table and leaned in a little menacingly. "It was four months ago and it was Garrett Blake." She straightened and shuddered. "He was a dork in high school and he's still a dork. Why did you go out with him again?"

Shelby shrugged.

"Shell...?" Laney prodded.

"Okay, fine. My parents set us up. They're friends with Garrett's folks and they thought we had things in common."

"The only thing the two of you had in common is you both live in Magnolia and you're both boring."

"Hey!" Shelby snapped, not even mildly amused.

"It's true! I'm not going to sugar coat it for you! You said you're in a rut, I agreed, and now we're going to fix it!" Coming around to Shelby's side of the table, she pulled her to her feet. "We are going out tonight and we're going to find you someone interesting to go out with!"

Shelby couldn't help it, she snorted with disbelief. "Good luck with that. The only guys who ever seem to be attracted to me are boring."

"Not where we're going."

Laney took Shelby's hand in hers and dragged her out of the break room, out of the library, and out to their cars. "Where are we going?"

Grinning, Laney nudged Shelby toward her car. "You're going to go home and find something fun to wear– not any of your librarian clothes," she clarified. "And we are going to take a ride to Wilmington and have dinner and go for a couple of drinks and go dancing. Then we're..."

The loud sound of lawn equipment flared to life and blocked out whatever it was Laney was going to say. Shelby looked over her shoulder and sure enough, the landscaping crew was next door cutting their neighbor's lawn. Part of her wanted to be annoyed, but...Sam Westbrook was the one on the large mower today and...*yum*.

Tall, sandy brown hair, stubbled jaw, tanned skin, and oh so many muscles that were currently on display as he walked around in a tight, white t-shirt and a pair of snug, well-worn jeans...yeah, a woman would have to be dead to not look at Sam and think all kinds of naughty thoughts.

I bet he tastes good too.

She let out a quiet little hum of approval as Laney stepped in beside her.

"Ahh...good to know it's not mutual."

Shelby turned her head so quick she felt a sharp pain in her neck. Rubbing at it irritably, she asked, "What are you talking about?"

"You just said how only boring guys are attracted to you." She shrugged. "I was beginning to wonder if that was all *you* were attracted to too." Then she nodded in Sam's direction. "I've heard Sam Westbrook described in many ways, and boring isn't one of them."

Yeah, Shelby had heard all about him too.

From just about everyone she knew.

Frowning, she forced herself to look away. "Yeah, well... it doesn't matter. I'd never go out with someone like Sam and I greatly doubt I'm his type either, so..."

Laney slapped her playfully on the shoulder. "Oh, stop. You don't know that."

Walking over to her car, she let out another sigh. "Trust me. I do. Any time I've ever been within five feet of Sam, it's like he sees right through me–like I'm not even there." She paused and hated how pathetic she sounded. "And why are we even talking about this? Don't we have plans or something?"

"We do! Just promise me something."

"Sure. What?"

"No glasses tonight. I know we already covered no librarian clothes, but that goes for the glasses to."

Reaching up, Shelby tentatively touched the frames. "You know these are just for show. They're not prescription or anything. I don't even need them."

"Then why do you wear them?"

This time her sigh was more of a huff. "We've been over this a thousand times; my parents don't know I got Lasik. They said it was a waste of money."

"Yeah, yeah, yeah...I know, but...your parents aren't here. I get why you'd wear them when you're out with them or over at their house, but...why all the time? You're going to have to tell them eventually."

"Oh, please. You know they'll give an endless lecture on how I shouldn't be so concerned about my looks and the importance of being wise with my money! And besides... basically everyone in this town has a big mouth," she said, frowning more. "You know if anyone we knew came into the library and saw me without my glasses, they'd ask why and then word would get back to my folks and...ugh. It's just easier this way. But don't worry, I won't wear them tonight."

"I'm serious, Shell, you are going to have to stand up to them. You can't keep living like this."

"I know, I know. And I will. Someday. Just...not today." She sighed and glanced one more time in Sam's direction. He was doing nothing but riding on the large mower and yet...he looked better than any man had a right to.

If only he'd look at me just once...

"Earth to Shelby."

Quickly, Shelby averted her gaze and muttered an apology. "So, um...yeah. No glasses tonight. No worries."

"Okay. Good. So go home and grab a change of clothes and then come to my place and we'll get ready." Then she stopped. "On second thought, just come home with me now."

"Why?"

"Because we both know you're going to bring something I'm going to disagree with and you'll ending up wearing something of mine anyway." She shrugged. "This just saves some time and then we'll have more time for dinner."

"I am completely on board with that because I am starving."

"You eat like a bird, Shell. Tonight, I'm putting my foot down and you will eat something more than a salad for dinner. You have to get a burger or at least a sandwich."

Inwardly, she cringed. "That's a very messy option and how productive would it be if I have ketchup stains all down the front of me when we hit a bar or club?"

Laney started to laugh and then nudged Shelby toward her car. "I know you hate eating anything with your hands so I'll give you a partial pass."

"A partial pass?"

"Uh-huh. No burgers or sandwiches, but you are eating something other than a salad. No arguments."

"Fine," she murmured and opened her car door. "I'll meet you back at your place."

"Sounds good."

Fifteen minutes later, they were going through Laney's closet in hopes of finding something cute for Shelby to wear. Normally she would protest, but deep down she knew Laney's wardrobe was far trendier than her own. And if she wanted to break out of this rut, some things had to change.

Like the way she dressed.

"I've got it!" Laney cried. Pulling down several hangers, she walked over to her bed and laid out her choice. "Black skinny jeans–you can never go wrong there." Then she pointed to a red, sleeveless silk shell. "We'll layer this with this super cute cropped cardigan. And I have an amazing red lace pushup bra you can wear under it! We're the same size and honestly, I bought it for myself for Christmas and never wore it so…" She was grinning from ear to ear. "What do you think?"

It wasn't horrible, but…

"I really don't look good in red. It's totally not my thing."

"And we're trying to break you of your things, so…you're wearing it."

That wasn't going to fly, so Shelby walked back over to the closet and began rummaging through until she found something a little more her style. "How about this?" She waved the hanger out the closet door. "It's still a shell and will work just the same."

"It's white, Shell," Laney replied wearily. "You need a pop of color!"

"Fine."

But it wasn't fine. It was stupid and annoying and Shelby had a feeling she was going to hate this entire night just based on one article of clothing. Stepping out of the closet, she looked at her friend with resignation.

"We'll go with the red, but if no one even talks to me or offers to buy me a drink, I'm blaming you *and* the shirt."

Laney jumped up and down excitedly, clapping her hands. "Yay! And trust me, you're going to look amazing and will have your choice of men by the end of the night!"

Shelby was still doubtful, but…something definitely had to give.

And if wearing a red top was the sacrifice she had to make, for tonight, she'd deal with it.

ABOUT THE AUTHOR

Samantha Chase is a New York Times and USA Today bestseller of contemporary romance. She released her debut novel in 2011 and currently has more than forty titles under her belt! When she's not working on a new story, she spends her time reading romances, playing way too many games of Scrabble or Solitaire on Facebook, wearing a tiara while playing with her sassy pug Maylene...oh, and spending time with her husband of 25 years and their two sons in North Carolina.

Where to Find Me:
Website: www.chasing-romance.com

Sign up for my mailing list and get exclusive content and chances to win members-only prizes!
http://bit.ly/1jqdxPR

 facebook.com/SamanthaChaseFanClub

twitter.com/SamanthaChase3

ALSO BY SAMANTHA CHASE

The Enchanted Bridal Series:

The Wedding Season

Friday Night Brides

The Bridal Squad

Glam Squad & Groomsmen

The Montgomery Brothers Series:

Wait for Me

Trust in Me

Stay with Me

More of Me

Return to You

Meant for You

I'll Be There

Until There Was Us

Suddenly Mine

The Shaughnessy Brothers Series:

Made for Us

Love Walks In

Always My Girl

This is Our Song

Sky Full of Stars

Holiday Spice

Tangled Up in You

Band on the Run Series:

One More Kiss

One More Promise

One More Moment

The Christmas Cottage Series:

The Christmas Cottage

Ever After

Silver Bell Falls Series:

Christmas in Silver Bell Falls

Christmas On Pointe

A Very Married Christmas

A Christmas Rescue

Life, Love & Babies Series:

The Baby Arrangement

Baby, Be Mine

Baby, I'm Yours

Preston's Mill Series:

Roommating

Speed Dating

Complicating

The Protectors Series:

Protecting His Best Friend's Sister

Protecting the Enemy

Protecting the Girl Next Door

Protecting the Movie Star

7 Brides for 7 Soldiers:

Ford

Standalone Novels:

Jordan's Return

Catering to the CEO

In the Eye of the Storm

A Touch of Heaven

Moonlight in Winter Park

Wildest Dreams (currently unavailable)

Going My Way (currently unavailable)

Going to Be Yours (currently unavailable)

Waiting for Midnight

Seeking Forever (currently unavailable)

Mistletoe Between Friends

Snowflake Inn